I0519752

THE KNOWN EXPERIMENT

THE KNOWN EXPERIMENT IS THE FIRST IN A SERIES OF EROTIC NOVELS BY THE AUTHOR OF THE POPULAR *SEX EXPERIMENT* BLOG.

FOR UPDATES ON THE TRUE EROTIC ADVENTURES OF MR. X AND HIS WIFE VISIT:

WWW.THESEXEXPERIMENT.COM

The Known Experiment

by Mr. X

An Experimental Book
www.experimentalbooks.com

The Known Experiment

Copyright © 2011 by The Sex Experiment Blog

Cover by: Kit Foster

All rights reserved. No part of this book may be reproduced in any form by any electronic or mechanical means including photocopying, recording, or information storage and retrieval without permission in writing from the author.

ISBN-13: 978-0-615-55119-7
ISBN-10: 0-615-55119-X

The Sex Experiment
www.thesexexperiment.com
Email: Books@thesexexperiment.com
Twitter: @sexexperiment

Printed in U.S.A

"You are one of The Known."

CHAPTER ONE

Katharine Bright's first e-mail left me wondering why she had sent it. She wrote that she had recently discovered The Sex Experiment blog, and that the sexual dares I had been giving my wife excited her tremendously. I expected her to ask for a dare of her own, as readers often did, but she just went on to tell me about herself in a way that was no more illuminating than a résumé.

She was twenty-eight years old and had grown up in Portsmouth, New Hampshire, she wrote. She'd always had boyfriends, smart boys from smart families with the right opinions and bright future. That was the way she put it, which was enough to indicate that she was looking for something else. These relationships always seemed to get serious fast, but then apparently everything in Katherine's life was like that. From an early age she had been on track towards the sort of comfortable life that her parents had lived, so that even the things she loved were meant to be made use of somehow. Ballet was her passion, at least up until puberty, and she dreamed as a girl does of dancing on famous stages in Paris and Moscow. She was a head taller than the other girls, and moved less limberly, but she practiced harder and loved the pain, because pain eventually transformed her into a beautiful bird moving freely through the air. Her mother never missed a recital and fully supported her "hobby" for the good it might eventually do on her college applications.

When she turned sixteen, Katharine stopped dancing. Seemingly overnight, her body was no longer a bird's. Maybe she had always been more like a stork than a swan, but now she was a woman. She found her body difficult to manage. Her instructor said her breasts and hips were too big, and as hard as she worked, they would always be a hindrance to any kind of serious career as a dancer.

So she quit to focus entirely on her studies, until in her senior year of high school she was accepted by every Ivy League school to which she had applied. She chose Brown, where in a required sophomore Art History course she rediscovered some of the joy she'd felt in dancing. Art was an opening to the world, and to freedom, just as ballet had been. She loved the Italian Futurists in particular, who at the turn of the century had written manifestos to speed, youth, and violence and had made powerful paintings with slashing colors. The Futurists made her feel like a rebel, and although sex wasn't a luxury she indulged in often, they turned her on. She graduated with a major in art history, the star of her department, but even then her parents weren't pleased, particularly when she decided to continue her art studies at Columbia. They had always wanted her to become a doctor or an engineer and thought she was throwing away her chances. But the Futurists had enabled her to form a rebellious thought or two, and she figured that she was finally giving herself a chance.

Katharine Bright was Doctor Bright by age twenty-eight, when she was awarded a fellowship to study the Futurists at the Getty Institute in Los Angeles. Under her parents' influence she had always thought of the West Coast as being slightly disreputable, if not vulgar, but not only did she love her work, she loved the sunshine – running through it down the beach every morning before diving under a wave, feeling it on her skin when she laid out on her balcony in a slightly tiny bikini. Men were impressed. The running and swimming kept her in perfect shape, and although she still stood out, it wasn't because she was gawky anymore. She was five-eleven with a tight waist and a 36 C bust. Her pale blonde hair fell past her shoulders, her brown eyes gave her a hint of mystery, and more than a few admirers had called her legs "endless". She recognized these qualities, if only in a clinical way. The only feature of hers she really hated were her lips, which were "pulpy", as a co-worker had put it – full and somehow lipsticked by nature – but she couldn't put a finger on why they embarrassed her so much.

She dated a few men – good-looking go-getters of the sort

she'd grown up with – with whom she would have sex after a while, mildly satisfying episodes during which each partner would politely and competently take care of the other's needs. You could have written cheery sex manuals on Katharine and her lovers. She laughed about it with girlfriends.

It was at a conference in San Francisco that she met Nicolas Lenoir. She had spotted him coming across the reception room towards her. He wasn't like the men she knew. He wore a dark blue suit with a dark blue tie and looked to be about forty, with gray at his temples that looked not like a sign of age, but a sign of some secret, privileged experience. He moved like a dancer, she thought, with controlled and fluid movements, and his eyes stabbed the room like shining daggers that he knew exactly how to wield. And then, and then, he told her that she was beautiful before he asked what she did. She blushed and responded by asking what he did. He was French (of course) and he made her feel too much like an American. The conference was about early twentieth-century art, and he was there to speak as a representative of his auction house in Paris, where he was a director. They talked for a while, Katharine feeling again like that storkish sixteen-year-old with ungainly tits and hips, and it was only that night when she got back to her hotel room and was soaping herself in the shower that she realized what a desire he had awakened. A finger slipped into her pussy and she came with a savage shout that frightened and embarrassed her.

The next evening she found herself at another cocktail party and found him moving gracefully across the room towards her again. He had a proposition to make, he said, and although she blushed again, she had already determined to accept. He had looked into her history, he said (at which an image of her wild shower orgasm came to her mind, and water streaming over her tits). She had done impressive research at the Getty, he continued, and he was curious to know if she would like to spend a year in Paris working for him and expanding her knowledge, as well as her contacts. If she agreed, she would be working directly under him as one of his two research assistants, authenticating pieces for the house.

Perhaps it was her disappointment in his strictly professional proposal, or perhaps it was because she had never done anything impulsive in her life, but she agreed on the spot. And then he didn't even propose a drink to celebrate. He had another meeting to attend. Katharine blushed again, and that night she showered like a practical girl, still embarrassed by the previous night's desire. Paris would be a good opportunity to perfect her French, she thought to herself, and the auction house would be an impressive addition to her résumé. And then with a surge of joy, in spite of what a fool she must have made of herself with Lenoir, she thought of the Paris Ballet, and of freedom, and of soaring lightly like a bird.

In her last weeks in Los Angeles, she put out the word on

Facebook: she was coming to Paris for a year, and any old college friends over there should definitely get in touch. They did, and only a week after arriving she was already well-surrounded by a social set that was a perfect forgery of the sets she had known in the States. They took her to the right restaurants and bars, and they all talked English together but ordered off the menu in French. It was on one of these nights that she met Michel, a thirty-five-year-old French lawyer who had studied in the States, hung around Americans when he could, and talked fondly of "the American system". He paid particular interest to Katharine, who found him both handsome and friendly, and she went home with him one night. Within a couple of months, she had moved into his spacious loft on the Rue de Seine in the chic neighborhood of Saint Germain. He worked long hours, so she was often alone, but he treated her well, and she had to admit that watching him order the right wine in a swank restaurant somehow turned her on. Not screaming orgasm stuff, but he wasn't the worst lover she'd had by any means. So she wasn't unhappy, but there was this: she'd stepped onto the track again, even in Paris, and there was a small part of her that wondered whether this meant that a freight train was coming along the track to mow her down. Had she taken enough time to consider her choices? Here she was living an almost identical life to the one she had lived in America, with almost identical friends, with just a bit of French sprinkled in. But she liked these friends, and she liked Michel, and most nights that was enough to put her to sleep.

The auction house was run by Monsieur Legrand, but to everyone besides Monsieur Legrand it was run by Nicolas. He was constantly on the phone, constantly in movement in his blue suit and tie, dazing like a hypnotist everyone he passed. Katharine would smile to herself at the way he made women swoon, at the way men struggled for words and swiped at the lint on their jackets when he engaged them in conversation. Then Nicolas' gaze would fall upon her, and she would swoon and struggle despite herself. She would think: this is a wonderful professional opportunity, and it's magical to be in the City of Lights. And she would return to her work even more assiduously, building a provenance for works of art as meticulously as the engineer her parents had wanted her to be. Then he invited her for a drink one evening, and she splurged for a taxi to race home and change into a slinkier dress with heels. Michel was still at work when she decided she wouldn't wear a bra.

Why did she feel as if Nicolas was always in the process of seducing her? Was she reading too much into his suavity? Wasn't seduction just in his nature, and wasn't he that way with everyone? She could ask herself these questions when she was alone, but around him she lost all perspective. He was the sort of man she knew so well in her dreams that when he appeared in person, just an arm's length away, she was as startled as she would have been if Humphrey Bogart had walked in and offered to buy her a whisky. And then he was always so complimentary, not only about her work, which she was accustomed to, but about her looks. He always noticed what she was wearing and never failed to compliment any little stylish touch that pleased him. That evening when she walked into the bar, he stood, handed her a glass of wine, looked her up and down (lingering, perhaps, on those tits that now felt naked), and said matter-of-factly: "You look ravishing in that dress."

She mustered her confidence and looked him in the eye to reply: "And you say that to all the girls."

"No I don't," he said, still deadly serious, meeting her gaze so intently that she could hardly stand it. Then he flashed that wild, infectious grin and said: "My life is about making distinctions, Katharine – between good and bad, or more often good and great. I would never call a bad Boccioni imitation good, and when I call you great in that dress I am making a distinction. Even greater out of that dress, I'm certain. You'd make a sculptor out of me." To which she blushed, dammit, and he roared with laughter, turning heads everywhere as he put his hand on hers. She quickly pulled it away and said with a smile she hoped was as sly as his: "Not so fast, mister." What the hell was she doing?

She drank a lot quickly. A half dozen luxurious women stopped by to leave lingering kisses on the cheeks of Nicolas, their eyes twinkling, first at him, then at her. She grew more anxious by the minute. She was out of her depth and wanted to go home. Now she felt him mocking her innocence, her American-ness, and she wanted to shock him, to make him think of her differently, but not by going to bed with him, because that wouldn't shock him at all. It was exactly what he expected. So she made her excuses soon enough and hailed another cab, leaving Nicolas between two beautiful women who made her furious. What a jerk he really was, when you thought about it. Her head was foggy with wine, but she was clear about that.

The next day at the office he was as amused with the world and as charming as ever, waltzing in (as ever) an hour after everyone else, while she felt stupidly hungover and glum. He had a painting he wanted her and Arnaud, his other research assistant, to look at in the stockroom, and said he'd meet them back there in a minute. She sighed to herself as Arnaud winked over from his desk. These French men. Take Nicolas, of course, but then take Arnaud: he was such a cretin that even fancy suits couldn't hide it. He was already balding, his face was always sheened with sweat, and he had a pretty, boring girlfriend who occasionally and timidly picked him up from work (Katharine thought with a certain mean satisfaction). Of course when the girlfriend wasn't around he would ooze all over anything with a skirt. Every other sentence the creep uttered was a bad pickup line. "I dreamed of you last night," he'd said to her one morning, and then had proceeded to stand there with a counterfeit Nicolas Lenoir grin on his face, fully expecting her to coyly ask what the dream had been about. "That's funny, Arnaud," she had said. "I dreamed about your girlfriend."

The stockroom was where they kept all the artworks they were researching for auction or storing for clients. It looked more like a museum than any ordinary stockroom, with cedar closets in which paintings were stored and large tables at which the researchers could work. Katharine and Arnaud went in and had a seat. He started to say something that had a seventy percent chance of being a pickup line. She didn't like her odds, so she gave him a warning look that shut him up, and he ran a hand through hair he didn't have. She didn't mind bald men. Bald men could be attractive, but on Arnaud hairlessness just looked like another failure.

As researchers their main job was to gather information about past owners and sales for any artworks set for auction, propose estimates, and flag anything that looked suspicious. They provided the background information for Nicolas, who had the eye. He truly was a virtuoso when it came to this. Katharine might spend a week poring through papers to be able to tentatively propose that a painting might be a fake, but Nicolas could spot a fake in an instant. He was the star, and everyone who knew anything in the art world knew that. She was just a grinder, she often thought to herself those days. She accumulated facts better than anyone, and could calculate answers as well as a machine. But she didn't have the magic. It had occurred to her that this unimaginative process was one that she had also applied to her actual life, and she wished that she could just look and feel and know like Nicolas.

"1901, Post-Impressionist, supposedly a student of Gauguin," Nicolas said as he pulled out a painting and gently slid it onto the table in front of them. It was of a dark-skinned man and woman fucking beneath a palm tree. You could see the length of the man's cock, hard and set to enter. You could even see the lips of the woman's pussy, which were slightly spread. Arnaud giggled, then coughed.

"Really 1901?" Katharine asked with a frown. "Look," Nicolas instructed, hovering over her shoulder. She inhaled his musky scent.

"Beautiful," Arnaud said curtly. "But I agree with Katharine. 1901?"

"Look at the woman's lips," Nicolas said, and so they did, Katharine trying to focus her attention on the lips and away from her breathing. The woman's head was thrown back in mad, blind lust, and her lips were impossibly full and red. "I hate to be the one to say it," Arnaud purred, "but those lips were made for you know what. The last time I saw lips like that was the last time Katharine was saying something disapproving, which I'm sure was about five seconds ago."

She hated him, but she blushed anyway. "You're an asshole, Arnaud," she said through clenched teeth, drawing her lips inward and hating herself, and her ridiculous lips, even more.

"There's some paperwork in the library," Nicolas smiled to Arnaud, who skipped off as if he'd just gotten laid.

Nicolas studied the painting then turned to her and appeared surprised that she was still seething. "Oh come on," he said. "So you have stunning, cock-sucking lips. There are worse fates for a woman."

"*Excuse* me?"

"Just look at the painting and tell me what you *see*. You need to learn to look, Katharine. You need to learn to feel instead of just thinking."

"Just stop, Nicolas. I have a boyfriend, you know, and I'm sick of pickup lines."

"You *need* to get picked up," he said with an inscrutable smile. "And I'd start by letting this painting do it to you." So she looked, and she looked, and despite herself she wished that she could see everything that he saw and understand everything that he was talking about. Also: the stockroom was kept cold and she knew that her nipples were hard.

In her e-mail to me there was also this abrupt and mysterious confession: she had been caught shoplifting a camisole out of Printemps, the big Parisian department store, and Michel had needed to call a few lawyer friends to keep her out of trouble. She'd been mortified. She had no idea why she'd done it, but the truth was that she'd been shoplifting little things for years, ever since she was a teenager. A magazine, a pair of cheap earrings, a candy bar she would never eat. The first time had been a bag of M&M's from a convenience store in Portsmouth at age fifteen. The shopkeeper had seen her take it, and when she walked out without paying he'd shouted and had taken off after her. She'd run off into the evening as fast as her long legs would take her, trembling with excitement, running and running, panic coursing through her veins like a drug, panic massing between the legs of her little cut-off shorts until the excitement became something even more extreme, something she'd never felt before. The shopkeeper was far behind her now. She stopped to collect herself and put a tentative hand between her legs. Later that night she realized she'd had her first orgasm, and then she took off her shorts and touched herself again. She put a finger inside, and it felt so good. How had she never known about this? She kept touching and playing until she got the trick and came again. After that she had a new hobby.

Had she kept shoplifting over the years in search of sexual excitement? She didn't think so. She hated herself for these little lapses, really, and she couldn't explain why she did them. It wasn't often – once or twice a year – and stealing seemed to take away the itch to steal for a while. Of course since she couldn't explain the impulse to herself, it had been impossible to explain it to Michel. "Well at least you were trying to look beautiful for me," he had said condescendingly, stroking her hair like a little girl's as she wept after his rescue. She felt angry and dumb and hated that he had seen her that way. She wished that she could be like one of those charming nymphettes in French movies who smoked cigarettes, broke laws, and discarded men.

As I read I kept asking myself why this woman was writing to me. I still had no idea. To be honest I was surprised that my sex blog had turned her on. She didn't seem the type. What was clear to me, however, was that she was looking for something, and so I wrote back, told her just that, and added that I'd be happy to help her find whatever she was missing if I could.

"Last night I took a long walk across the Seine and past the Madeleine," she wrote back without further introduction. "I've been masturbating all the time, and I wanted to see the place where the sex shops are." A promising start, I had to admit. Maybe this Katharine was my kind of woman after all. Michel was working every night, seven nights a week, and maybe it was because spring was in the air and the nights were warm, but after work alone at home she could hardly keep her hands from her pussy. She'd found a dance studio in the Marais that offered classes twice a week and had signed up for one with a sort of defiance. That helped a bit. She would dance and dance until she was exhausted, relishing the chance to push her body that way again. She was still extremely flexible, she'd found, and after a few weeks of class she was moving as easily as ever. She wanted to exhaust herself. On nights when she didn't have class, she danced at home, looking out the large windows of Michel's loft to the offices across the Rue de Seine. She danced, and she sweat, and she showered and masturbated and squeezed her nipples until they hurt and she came. Sometimes she would go out walking, and this one night she headed towards the Madeleine. She wasn't out to steal anything - she had no desire to take that risk again - but her heart beat wildly as if that was her intention.

"Do you know that on a side street off the Madeleine whores sit dressed up in fancy cars waiting for clients? Apparently they'll drive them off to apartments or suck their dicks in the back seat." She was fascinated by these women, fascinated by their lives and the logistics of paying for sex in Paris. Was it because they made her feel dirty – or clean by comparison? – that she found the nerve to walk into the sex shop? That had been her destination all along – there were several along that street, just a couple of blocks over from the site of her shoplifting disgrace – but she didn't guess she'd ever really intended to enter one when it came down to it. But she had. The scary part had been the entering. Once she was inside she wasn't scared at all. The place was clean, the shopkeeper paid her no particular attention, and she began to browse. That was the night she bought her first vibrator. It was no bigger than a cigarette lighter and made her come in fifteen seconds flat. So far the record was six times in a night. She was keeping it hidden in the bottom of one of her drawers, but she hardly needed to bother with that. Michel didn't have that kind of curiosity about her, she knew. He didn't understand secretiveness because he had nothing to hide. And she realized that this (although she loved him, sure) was not entirely a compliment.

"I want a dare, Mr. X," she wrote. "I don't know what I'm doing, but I want you to make me do more."

After that we began to write each other regularly. I initially proposed to her the first experiment that I had proposed to my wife on the blog: she was to go out without bra or panties and see what happened. She was to look at men – fearlessly – to find the ones she liked, and she was to pay particular attention to their reactions to her body. Would they suspect her nakedness? How much would she reveal? How far was she really willing to go? She accepted my challenge and wrote that she would get back to me with the results of the experiment as soon as possible. And so I waited, imagining a tall blonde with impossibly long legs, kissing lips, and tits meant to be studied like artwork.

In the meantime she continued her walks through the Paris night, now *sans* bra or panties. Although she'd always hated the lascivious stares of men, now she forced herself to give into their stares, and to eventually stare back. She even went out and bought – yes, bought – a few short skirts to show off her legs, which had lost their L.A. tan but were in perfect shape again from the dancing. She loved the feel of fresh air on her cunt, so close to exposure, and sometimes she had to concentrate on other things to keep from furtively touching herself right there on the sidewalk. And the feel of her bare thighs brushing ever so slightly against each other? Just that alone could almost make her come.

Her tops got more daring too. More precisely, she made her conservative buttoned shirts more daring by undoing an extra button…or two. She had cleavage, she was proud to inform me, and her tits were honestly so perky that they really didn't need a bra. She liked to undo the buttons until the firm, round tops of her breasts were revealed, and although it took her a while to find the confidence, she learned to walk with her head held high and her tits thrust out, at least at night. During the day she dressed as conservatively as ever and felt like another person. This person felt safer, but she wasn't sure she liked her as much.

One night she sat down at a big sidewalk café at Maubillon, not far from Michel's loft, and ordered a glass of white wine. She drank the wine fast and looked around for something else to do. She was wearing her shortest skirt, her ass almost out onto the wicker seat of her chair. Her legs were crossed. She uncrossed them, keeping her knees close together. She wondered what Nicolas would think of her now, and smiled. She spread her knees slightly, and watched the passersby. Men walking alone were the only ones at whom she would dare returning a stare. When they came in pairs they always seemed to feel the need to perform their lust for her to each other, and this made her uncomfortable.

Now there was a man in a sports jacket and open shirt crossing towards her from the south side of the Boulevard Saint Germain. She spread her knees a little further, and with the tip of a finger she eased the skirt a half an inch up her thigh. The man's eyes had picked her out, she noticed, and then she couldn't look anymore. Was he handsome? She had no idea.

But she spread her knees further anyway, looking down at the sidewalk, her hair falling over her face. Her pussy was now exposed, she knew, and she could hardly stand it. Her heart raced wildly. She was dizzy, she needed another drink, but she was determined to hold on for a moment longer. And she did…then crossed her right leg over her left again, feeling a delicious smudge of wetness between them. Then she steeled herself yet again, to look up shyly at the man who was now passing by. He wasn't looking at her, but he had a smile on his face, as if savoring a private thought of his own. She found herself desperately wanting to know whether he'd seen her and wishing she'd held on for a moment longer. He wasn't bad looking either.

The next night, with Michel still at work as always, she casually stripped to her underwear in front of the windows of the loft. She did some stretching, trying her best to seem nonchalant and watching the lights from the offices across the street out of the corner of her eye. Her pussy was wet again. As timid as she typically was, at that moment she wanted to fuck the night. She ran off to the bedroom, giggling at her own horny absurdity, and dug out the vibrator, and came three times in succession while imagining that she'd been seen. What turned her on most that night was the thought of the image of her almost naked body in other people's brains.

The next night she danced topless, her tits bobbing as she stretched and leapt across the room, barefoot in her flesh-colored tights. She felt like a finely-tuned physical specimen, and even the soles of her feet were like erogenous zones as they slapped across the wooden planks of the floor, then across the carpet and through the air. She went *en pointe* and stretched her arms high in the air, feeling the satisfying pull in her shoulders as she reached up to the whole impressive length of herself, her breasts rising like sunflowers to nod up at the ceiling. And then, holding the pose, she forced herself to look out the windows at the building across the street. A few last workers moved from desk to desk under fluorescent lights, apparently too stressed by deadlines to notice nude dancers. But then, down towards the end of the block, she saw the silhouette of a man at a window. He was resting a hand on a vacuum cleaner – maybe one of the cleaning staff – and although she couldn't see his face clearly, he appeared to be looking directly at her.

She danced some more, for herself and the delirious erotic pleasure that the movements themselves gave, and she danced for the man in the window, perspiration beginning to shine on her shoulders and breasts. She danced hard until she was exhausted and flopped into an armchair, closing her eyes for a moment to savor the satisfying warmth in her muscles. Then she opened her eyes, and the man was still at the window. She quickly glanced away. *So let him see me*, she thought to herself with a giggle. This whole thing – these *experiments* – were completely ridiculous, but when was the last time she'd had so much fun?

So she stood and languidly stretched her body. She turned her back to the windows, hooked a thumb into each side of her tights, and bent slightly to peel them from her pale, toned ass. She peeled them over her strong thighs, past her knees, bending more and more, until the tights were down at her ankles and she kicked them off to stand fully and gloriously revealed in front of the window.

This was her great victory, she wrote to me. She felt as if in that act of stripping she had overcome many of the fears that had been haunting her for years. Her little performances had been stupid, she knew, and maybe dangerous too, but they had been so…fucking…exhilarating. I wrote back excitedly, telling her that visions of her naked body had taken up permanent residence in my brain, as if I'd been the man at the window. I praised her daring and asked if I might anonymously share some of her adventures with my readers. She didn't write back. She had disappeared.

For months I didn't hear from Katharine. I thought of her dancing at her window. I sent worried e-mails but never received a response.

Until one day I did. Something dramatic had happened over the past few months, she wrote, ever since we had begun experimenting together, and over the next weeks I received e-mail after e-mail – long, passionate letters describing an adventure more elaborate than anything I could have ever devised and a transformation in Katharine that was astonishing. As her story unfolded, I could hardly think of anything else. Day and night, I checked constantly for new e-mails, and when finally, *finally!*, I saw her name in my inbox, my cock would begin to stir in anticipation. I devoured her letters, again and again, and then between letters I would pester her with questions and beg for clarifications, desperate to get even deeper into the mind of this fascinating woman. At times I feared for her safety, and I thought rashly of flying to Paris, or – ridiculously – of calling the French police, but of course she would remind me that the dangers had passed, and that this was the story of a Katharine she hardly recognized anymore. So I would content myself with waiting for the next e-mail, and the next, until the whole, thrilling story was finally revealed to me.

What follows is Katherine's story in its entirety, assembled from her many e-mails and from her astonishingly open responses to my persistently lusty questioning. My hope is that I will be able to tell the story of her sexual adventures with as much explicit honesty as she told it to me, and that in putting it down I can somehow make sense of an obsession that still consumes me.

CHAPTER TWO

O n the night of Bastille Day, Thursday, July 14, 2011, Katharine Bright stood drinking expensive champagne at the window of the Paris loft of her boyfriend Michel. More accurately: she stood *through* the window, the glass of champagne held out over the Rue de Seine and her blonde hair whipping in the breeze. She was trying to get a glimpse of the fireworks that were being shot up over the Seine for French Independence Day. Most were bursting over the Eiffel Tower, which was far enough west of her that even hanging out the window she could only really see diffuse flashes of color in the sky. The explosions could be heard across the city, however, and that put her in a festive mood, even if she was drinking alone. She thought of that old song on the radio that had always made her father laugh: *When I drink alone, I prefer to be by myself.* He liked to make fun of country music, and it was a joke they shared, but now that line made perfect sense to her, and she sang it out to the street as the fireworks boomed in the distance. A man who had been lingering on the street below seemed to turn his head to hear her song, and she waved, but he was already gone.

Michel had popped out to his parents' house further up the

Boulevard Saint Germain for a quick glass of champagne. *Popped out.* He loved to use Americanisms like that, which always slightly embarrassed her. She'd begged off from the walk over to the "inlaws". She'd met them several times before (Michel had been quick to define their relationship...but then so had she), and she liked them, but tonight, she'd said, she was tired. This had bothered him, she could tell, but then she really couldn't be bothered. She couldn't tell him the truth, which was that she wasn't tired at all. In fact, over the past few weeks she'd hardly ever felt more awake or more alive. The truth was that she was thinking about Nicolas Lenoir and wanted to be left alone.

She had gone out for a drink with him again. He'd caught her as she was leaving the office the previous evening and had asked if she had time for a quick cocktail to discuss an upcoming auction before the long weekend. She had agreed, maybe a little too eagerly, but then who was she kidding? A large part of her was disgusted by him, by his sexual confidence, by the dozens of women who clearly adored him, but then there was that other large part of her that wasn't. And also, she admired his professional talent. She had never met anyone who knew so much about art, and was so sure of what he knew. She had learned more from him than she had ever expected to learn in her months in Paris, even if there were several aspects of the job she hated, specifically the odious Arnaud. And Nicolas...he really was unfailingly charming...though of course "international playboy" would never, ever, be her type.

"I like your hair up like that," he'd said as they sipped wine. Then his phone rang, as it always did, and she was left to look foolishly around the bar, seeing the salacious thoughts of others whose eyes she met. *Nicolas Lenoir has bagged himself another one. The poor, innocent thing doesn't know what she's getting herself into.* Yes, the phone call gave her the time and the space to get angry at her boss again.

They stayed at the bar for less than an hour before he had to run off to another appointment, and again he surprised her by talking strictly of business. There were clients who needed to be called, and he wanted her advice on how to "frame" the coming sale. This was what she was good at, and she lost herself in the discussion, pulling a pen from her purse to make quick little notes on a cocktail napkin. By the time they had agreed on how to proceed, she had drunk three glasses of wine and felt a bit tipsy as she deposited her pen back in her purse.

"It shows off the line of your neck," he said, settling back in his chair with a smile.

"I assume we're back to my hair," she said down to the table, chuckling despite herself. He said nothing, so she raised her eyes to meet his, which were happily shining. She couldn't help but smile. "You're doing wonderful work, Katharine, and I hope you're enjoying it here. You know if there's anything I can help you with outside of work, anything you might need, I'm happy to. I want you to get everything you possibly can out of your life here, and sometimes I feel that you're not, that something's bothering you."

She looked up at him again, and then the strangest thing happened: she found herself telling him about the shoplifting incident at Printemps, and how it had mortified her so, and how she wasn't like that, but how a force she couldn't understand had made her steal. She told him about Michel's reaction, and wondered aloud whether he'd been too kind – as if he'd known the incident would secure him some kind of future advantage. "I don't know why I'm telling you all of this," she said with a blush, as inside she screamed: *Why the hell are you telling him this?!*

Nicolas looked at her calmly, as if shoplifters confessed themselves to him nightly, and said: "Well if you get caught again, call me first."

"I won't *do* it again," she said, rolling her eyes.

"Did it give you a rush?" he asked, waving for the check.

She thought for a moment, put a hand to the bare "line of

her neck", then looked up into his handsome face and softly said: "*Yes.*"

He smiled, threw some money down on the table, and leapt to his feet. "I'm late," he said, stopping beside her to affectionately run a knuckle down her neck, which sent a tremor all the way down to her toes. Then he was calling out a goodbye, and he was gone, and she was left sitting there, feeling foolish and frustrated and watched by a dozen nosy people who thought they'd figured her out. "*Well they haven't,*" she hissed under her breath, and then the hisses turned to curses inside for losing her head and revealing too much to Nicolas Lenoir. Jerk. Dancing off like Baryshnikov. She wondered where he'd been going, and if he'd had a date, and then she cursed herself some more.

The fireworks were over now. It was almost midnight, and Michel still wasn't home. His mother had likely charmed him into another drink, Katharine thought as she moved away from the window. He had an unattractive tendency to be charmed by his mother, or his work, or whatever else made him feel like a good little boy. *That's unfair*, she thought, just as the phone rang. She skipped over to it, happy with champagne and prepared to say something coy and flattering to Michel. Maybe she could get him home and into bed.

But it wasn't Michel's voice on the line. It was that other voice, the one that spent too much time saying too many things in her head. "Katharine, it's Nicolas, I need your help." Great. That's what you get for being chatty. Your louche boss starts to call you any hour of the night, and on a holiday.

"Nicolas," she said, her voice rising in anger. "It's midnight on Bastille Day."

"I know Katharine, and I'm sorry, but I need you to listen carefully." He was deadly serious, she realized from the tone of his voice, and this had nothing to do with the previous night. "First of all, this absolutely has to stay between us," he said quickly. "I have to trust you, Katharine, and to be honest I'm not sure there's anyone one else I *can* trust."

"Of course," she said softly.

"Something has happened at work. A rare book was stolen from the vault last night, and Monsieur Legrand suspects that I had something to do with it."

"Nicolas! How could he *ever…*"

"Just listen. Supposedly my keycard was used to access the vault, and it's true that now I can't find it. So Monsieur Legrand suspects me. Of course it wasn't me, but this could be bad, Katharine. It could mean my job, but it could also mean the police if I don't figure out what actually happened. Right now it's not in Legrand's interest to bring in the authorities and draw attention to our security, but if this book doesn't turn up soon, he will. He won't have any choice."

The book was a rare Kama Sutra ("Appropriate, *n'est-ce pas?*" he said with a rueful laugh), and he had an idea of who might have been able to pull off such a sophisticated theft, but he needed time and he needed help. Thankfully they had a long weekend, but he probably wouldn't be back in the office on Monday. He was going to go into "hiding" for a while until the situation was resolved.

"What can I do, Nicolas?" she asked. "This isn't you. I'll do anything. Who is this person you suspect? Someone in the office? A client?"

"I'll worry about that," he said. "What I need from you is confirmation of my alibi. That should at least get me off the hook with Legrand – and the police if it goes that far."

"Just tell me what to do," she said, so urgently that her lips touched the phone, leaving a smudge of red.

"Last night I left you because I was expected at a gallery opening on Rue Mazarine. According to Legrand, the vault was accessed just after 9:30, and there's no doubt that at more or less that time I was standing looking at a photograph of a woman."

"Nicolas!" she groaned. "How is that an alibi? *I was looking at a photograph of a woman?*"

"Listen to me, Katharine. Listen to me now. A funny thing happened. I really admired this photograph. I was even thinking that I might buy it. It's of a woman, a nude, and you and I have both seen a million of them, but there was a certain *strangeness* to it, a beauty found from a new angle, and I just couldn't stop looking. Then, as I was standing there, I felt someone standing next to me, and I turned, and I could hardly believe my eyes: it was the woman in the photograph. As beautiful as expected. Even more. So we began to talk about nothing in particular, just a bit of flirtation, and then she was called away by someone else. I didn't get her name. I don't even know who took the photograph."

"Well well," she said, disguising her concern with sarcasm. "What a typically Nicolas Lenoir story."

"Isn't it," he sighed, ignoring the sarcasm. "So I need you to go over to the gallery, figure out who the woman is, and find her. Then, if I can't fix this as I think I can, I'll at least have an alibi in place when it gets ugly. I hate to drag you into this mess, Katharine…but can you do this for me?"

"Of course, Nicolas," she said, then helplessly: "I'll do anything."

He gave her the address of the gallery, and told her where to find the photograph. "The photos are all nudes, by the way. I'll be curious to hear what you think."

"Ha. Ha. Are you always so cool when you're on the run?"

"I'm not cool, Katharine," he said softly. "But I wanted to hear you laugh. Now I'm going away for a bit. You may not hear from me for a few days, but I'll be in touch soon, and hopefully by then you'll have some information on our mysterious woman. And *please*, Katharine. Nobody knows about this conversation but us."

"Okay, Nicolas," she said, suddenly scared. She wanted to hear him say something more, but he'd already hung up.

More champagne, now without fireworks or joy. Dark emotions overwhelmed her – the feeling that she'd been caught at something bad again – and she wanted to act immediately. She wanted to run out into the night and bang on the doors of the gallery, but that was foolish, so instead she just drank. Eventually she took off her clothes and went to bed, but she left the light on and kept drinking.

Michel came in not long afterwards, singing *La Marseillaise*.

"*Aux Armes, Citoyens!*" He was in a good mood, and she almost smiled. "Good time?" she asked when he appeared in the bedroom doorway, grinning at her and her body.

"Good time," he sighed, and began to take off his clothes. There was nothing she could do for Nicolas now, she thought to herself, and she liked to look at Michel naked. In his work clothes, which were his only clothes, he always looked castrated somehow, too boxed in and tied up. But as his shirt came off, she studied his powerful arms. He worked out every day at lunch, and it showed. His chest was skinnier than his arms, and a bit hairless for her taste, but it looked right on him. His charm was his boyishness. Then his pants came off, his socks. She liked his legs. He had exercises for them, and they looked powerful. Cute ass, too. Nice and full and firm, such that even when he was wearing those awful weekend French jeans of his, she often couldn't resist pinching it. His underwear came off, and his dick came out – it was the first uncircumcised one she had ever seen, and it had scared her at first, but then she had grown to like it, possibly because it was the one thing about him that had scared her. Plus, uncircumcised it looked bigger, and sometimes she let herself imagine that she was being taken by a blunt savage. Not that Michel was ever a blunt savage.

"Let's leave the light on tonight," he said as he whipped the sheet from her lap, revealing the wisps of blonde hair at her pussy and her magnificent legs, stretching endlessly down to her toes, which she had painted earlier that evening in a dark red. "Not tonight," she said, and shut off the light.

She did like the feel of him on top of her, though, and when he moved towards her she spread her legs to keep him there. He worked a finger diligently across her clitoris as she kissed him deeply and tried to forget herself. On his tongue she tasted a cigarette, which he would regret in the morning as a setback to his health program, but she found that the taste turned her on, and she let a hand slide down his tensed arm, over his belly, rippled with muscle, until she found the head of his dick and ringed it with her index finger and thumb. Lightly, she began to move her fingers up and down, moving his foreskin back and forth so that it clicked over the swell of his head, and quickly he was hard down the width of her hand and whispering sweet things in her ear. He had eased the tip of a finger inside her now, and she was growing wet around it as she stroked harder at his dick. "Just fuck me," she hissed into the darkness.

"Well *okay*," she heard him say, and then it was blissfully silent until he pierced her deeply and she shattered the silence with a primordial groan. "Just fuck me," she said again, and closed her eyes even to the darkness. Only then did she begin to see things.

As her newly red-painted nails raked the wide, flat muscles of

Michel's back, it was Nicolas she was pulling into her, feeling his lithe limbs wrapping around her, feeling his cock – yes, his *cock* – she wanted to scream the word – pressing deeply into what was now a sea of wet. She grasped Michel's ass with both hands, hard, and it was Nicolas - fucking charming, seductive Nicolas - whom she was pulling so deeply inside that he would touch a place in her that had never been touched. Oh! "*Fuck me!*" she hissed, this from a woman who had never before uttered anything in bed other than a timid *Yes*. Michel's tongue was at her throbbing nipples, and she wanted Nicolas to bite them. Bite her! She wanted to bleed for him. In that moment, at least, she wanted him everywhere, his cock everywhere, pressed against her skin in a hundred different places, and swelling, and swelling, until he came like a typhoon all over her pale white skin. One of her hands was at her clitoris now, pawing furiously at it and feeling Michel pump in and out of her like a piston. The other hand she dropped to her other nipple, and she pinched it hard but held her tongue, because she feared the word she would scream was: *Nicolas!*

Michel was swelling inside of her now, and she knew he was about to come. She heard the rasp of his breathing, and as he pumped and pumped towards the end, she was returned to herself, and she was embarrassed for Michel, but mostly for herself. And then, with one last clench of his thighs, it was over and the slickness inside her was now his come. Quickly he rolled over onto his back and giggled to himself. "You *wanted* it. Didn't you, you little monster?"

She blushed up into the darkness, wondering soberly now whether it had just been the champagne, or if there was something seriously wrong with her head. She just wanted to sleep and forget about absolutely everything, so she looked up at the ceiling she couldn't see, and said: "Yes."

Tomorrow was another day, and Michel would of course work, and she would walk into a gallery on the Rue Mazarine, a sunny modern space with large plate glass windows looking out onto the street. A loft overhung one end of the room, separated by a railing of metal cables stretched tight, and there appeared to be a desk and couches up there. And then, in the corner of the ground floor, underneath the loft, just as Nicolas had instructed, was the photograph of the woman whom she had been asked to find. She was indeed naked, except for a silver pocket mirror that she held in front of her darkly angled face and which hid precisely nothing. Her skin was dark – Latin – and Katharine had rarely seen curves so perfect. Her black hair was curled down over her shoulders, so that she looked like a fabulous pinup model from the 1950's. Nicolas had been right. There was a *personality* there, a vibrancy so powerful that Katharine couldn't take her eyes from the photograph.

But she knew she had a job to do, and that job made her so

nervous that she'd hardly slept the night before. For a moment, however, she could do nothing but stare and stare. That was one beautiful woman, and she cringed at the thought of Nicolas chatting her up, just as he chatted up everyone else. The thought made her miserable, but she took a deep breath and told herself that the man was only her boss and she was simply doing her job, just as she would write a press release.

Doing her best to look like a dispassionate collector of art (whatever that looked like), she efficiently browsed for a bit until a woman she assumed was the owner approached, pegged Katharine for an American, and introduced herself in English as "Harriet, just Harriet". Harriet just Harriet was about forty and wore an angular black dress cut above the knee that looked as if it had been designed by some Danish designer with a theory. She was as angular as the dress, thin and deeply tanned, with sharp, high cheekbones, flat, compact breasts, and curly black hair cut short to her head like a Roman emperor. Her eyes were as black as her hair, and they scared Katharine. There was no hint of play in them, nor was there in her mouth, which was thin and lined with lipstick so deeply red that it was almost black itself. Harriet just Harriet was exotic-looking in a way Katharine knew she wasn't, and maybe this scared her too. Not that the woman was unattractive. She could have been the thinner older sister of the woman in the photograph, the sister with the business mind but without the voluptuousness. There was something almost

Indian about her – American Indian – and images of hatchets and desert campfires flashed through Katharine's mind. There was something that scared her about that too.

"I'd like to know more about the woman in the photo in the corner over there," Katharine said. "The one holding the mirror." Harriet nodded crisply, then took a moment to look Katharine over from head to toe, as if she was the object for sale.

"It's an edition of twenty five prints, and each one is selling for five thousand euros. Let me get you a price list."

"No," Katharine blurted out. "I'm looking for the *woman*, actually. A friend of a friend…and so forth…."

Harriet looked her over again, this time with the hook of a smile on her mouth, lingering on Katharine's legs and breasts as if they might clear up the mystery of the request.

"I'm sorry, but I don't deal with models," Harriet said coolly as her eyes met Katharine's and flashed almost imperceptibly with a dark, volcanic fire. "I deal with photographers."

Katharine cursed herself. Of course this woman wouldn't personally know the subjects in all of the photographs she sold. Again, she felt like an inexperienced fool. It was becoming a familiar feeling. "Well do you know where I could find the photographer?" she asked quickly, and then blushed as she thought: *I sound like a petulant child.*

"I handle his business affairs," Harriet said, seemingly more delighted by the second. "So if it's about his art, you're better off talking to me."

But it wasn't, Katharine explained. He was a friend of a friend, sort of, and she needed to pass along a message – nothing to do with his art, really – and she just needed to pass along this message in person. That was important – in person. Harriet's smile widened with every syllable, and although Katharine had decided that she hated the woman, she also decided that she might be very beautiful. She had a real dancer's body, the straight-lined body that Katharine had never had. She walked over to a desk near the entrance, her pointed heels stabbing the cement floor with a violence. The back of her dress was revealed, and it was cut away down to the top of her ass. Her back was as deeply tanned as the rest of her, and her shoulder blades protruded sharply on either side of the hard, dimpled column of her spine. At the desk she deftly kicked at a bottom drawer, making Katharine jump. The drawer ricocheted open, and Harriet bent to pull out a pad of paper, on which she wrote an address. "His name is John Salt," she said. "Another American."

"*Thank you,*" Katharine sighed, taking the paper. "And if you don't mind – you've already been so nice – could I leave my number…and could you just call me if anyone wants to buy the photograph, or if by any chance I can't contact this Mister Salt and you *do* come across the woman?"

"Of course," Harriet said, her smile now radiant – too radiant, Katharine thought as she nervously fumbled in her purse for a business card, then thought better of revealing her place of work to this woman and sheepishly reached for the pad on the desk. "Well *thank* you," she said, smiling brightly as she wrote down her name and number, doing her best friendly, naïve American act.

"Thank *you*," Harriet purred, and Katharine kept smiling and smiling and got out of there as fast as she could.

The address was on a side street just north of the Boulevard de Clichy. Katharine took the Metro to Pigalle and walked west, glancing occasionally to her right to look for the white dome of Sacre-Coeur, which would appear up the hill in the distance. The beauty of it allowed her to forget about her mission for a moment, and she thought of how much she really did love Paris. Every neighborhood was its own world, rich with architecture and beauty, and she never tired of discovering new ones. She smelled the summer air as the wind teased the edge of her simple white sundress, which she was wearing that day with some strappy leather sandals she'd found at a

Sunday flea market.

John Salt was nothing like what she had expected. She had pictured a fashion type, wanly pale and finicky about his dress – maybe affecting an ascot, unconscious of the clichés of an American artist in Paris. Instead he looked more like an un-kempt bar brawler who drove a beat-up truck and whose only connection to the grand Parisian school of Impressionism was the way he cut his hair. Dark blond and mashed about, it looked as if he cut it with a knife. He was barefoot and wore baggy, ripped blue jeans and a stained black t-shirt. "Come on in," he said distractedly as he ripped open the door and impatiently waved her in, seemingly without having set eyes upon her, much less asking who she was or why she was there.

"There" was a side of Paris Katharine hadn't seen. It was a shab-by building on a shabby street around the corner from a couple of shabby strip clubs where shabby girls stood handing out fly-ers in spangled bikinis. Salt's place was on the ground floor and was accessed from the street through a dented metal door. Once inside, she realized that the place must have once been a garage. Against a large metal door were stacked dozens of large, framed photographs and broken spars of metal equipment. Dusted out windows ran across the top of the garage door, let-ting in a pale yellow light. The floors were concrete, and as Salt led her into the center of the room, whose walls were covered with framed nudes, she saw a large mattress on the floor with a sheet thrown over it and doorway that she assumed (hoped?) must lead to a bathroom. Or maybe it was just a darkroom. John Salt obviously wasn't one for creature comforts.

"Sit down," he barked, clearing a stack of books from a chair and patting the seat gently as if softening it for her delicate behind. He'd taken the time to look at her by now, and as he patted the chair he wore a friendly grin. She dutifully sat, and seeming pleased with their progress so far, he bounded over to a high metal table, grabbed a bottle of Jim Beam, eyed two glasses in the dim light and decided they were clean, then poured out two glasses with a flourish. "Mother's milk," he muttered, handing her a glass. He downed his fast, standing almost on top of her, then vigorously shook his head as if he was emerging from deep water. "Mother's milk," he muttered again, and so she sipped hers half down, unable to repress a smile. Then he was off again, pulling photos out of the stacks, presumably for her to see. He had to be in his upper thirties, but he had the energy of an eighteen-year-old football player.

"My name is Katharine," she said across the room. "Pleasure, Katharine," he said as he rummaged, as if nothing could interest him less. Laughing, she said: "And I hope you're John Salt, because otherwise I'm in the wrong place and I've just drunk a stranger's bourbon."

He turned to face her and stared so long that the smile faded from her face. "I'll take a few candid shots first just to get us nice and relaxed, and then you can take off your clothes. I think this is going to be good."

"Oh no," Katharine cried, blushing. "I'm not...uh...here to model. It's kind of a crazy story, but I'm actually here looking for one of your...actual...models."

"Come here," he said impatiently, waving her over as if he was herding an errant sheep. "Look at these." So she rose, placed her empty glass back on the table, and walked over to where John Salt stood. Putting his hand to the small of her back, he positioned her in front of a black and white photograph almost as tall as she was. Another nude, this one of a perfectly muscled black man with his arms spread wide and his fingers flared, as if he was about to embrace her. It was a powerful photograph, but she wasn't thinking in terms of aesthetics just yet. What she was thinking was: *Look at the size of that cock*. Rock hard, terrifyingly thick, and extending halfway up the man's notched abdomen, it was so formidable that it appeared to leap off the photograph towards her into three dimensions. "What do you think of him?" she heard Salt ask, as if from a long distance away.

She turned and was surprised to find him still standing right next to her. "Well," she said, "the photograph is incredibly... powerful...and the subject is...well..."

"I asked what you think of *him*. Forget the photograph. That was just a moment, but I'm talking about the big picture."

Katharine rolled her eyes. "Well. He is…impressive."

"Good," Salt said quickly, as if she'd removed some doubt that had been bothering him. Then he put his hand to the small of her back again and took her from photograph to photograph. Every cock was huge, *unnaturally* huge (weren't they?), and every woman had curves and looked fearless. None of them was the woman with the mirror.

"She always screamed out lines of Rimbaud's when she came," he said of one. "How could you not fall in love with that?"

"And you've *fallen in love* with every one of them," she said sarcastically.

"Of course," he said matter-of-factly. "How could you not."

"Listen, John Salt, these are wonderful, truly, but I'm here for something else. I need to find another model of yours. She's in the show on the Rue Mazarine right now, and she's holding a mirror."

"Anita," he said distractedly, pulling out another photograph for her to see. "Haven't seen her in months. And you and every heterosexual male on the planet are looking for her."

"Well could you…."

"Quiet now. Look at that." He was like a kid admiring his own drawing on the refrigerator door, and she couldn't help but like him and admire his prodigious talent, even if he did push her beyond the limits of comfort. For example: the photo they now stood before was of a beautiful Asian woman being fucked from behind. The focus was on her face and its grimace of ecstasy. As the woman's body receded into the background it went out of focus, and the man standing behind her with his hands on her hips was an indistinct blur. But Katharine recognized him, and his wild hair, and she knew it was John Salt.

"What interests me as an artist are people," he said softly. She felt his animal presence moving closer, his breath at her cheek, and she felt her face growing hot, but she could not take her eyes from the photograph. "Photographs are just technique. Just moments. Anita is a friend of mine. Maybe I could help you find her, but I'd have to know you first, and to know you I'd have to photograph you. That's how I work. I'm loyal to her, and I'd need to have loyalty to both of you. I would need to know you."

This was interrupted by the sound of the metal door

slamming, and he cried: "Selena's here!" Another woman had entered the room. Katharine looked around in utter confusion. All she had to do was find this woman Anita, and that was it, but this strange man…and now this strange woman, Selena, kissing her on the cheek. Shorter than Katharine by a head, her ample tits were almost spilling out of her low-cut tank top, and her trashy turquoise skirt was so short that looking at her you could only think of sex. Katharine had already seen her naked, she realized, lying on a bed with her pelvis arched towards the camera in a photograph. Very sexy. She looked South American and confirmed the possibility by greeting Katharine with a hearty *Hola!*

"Perfect timing, Selena," Salt said nodding his head, beginning to bustle about again. "I need you to set up the camera. We're going to do a few shots of Katharine."

"No we are *not!*" Katharine said incredulously, finally returned to herself. Salt abruptly stopped his preparations and turned to her with a look of genuine surprise. Then he walked over, affectionately took her hands in his, and softly said: "Katharine, you are beautiful, and I very much want to photograph you. I promise that I will not touch you, and I promise not to show whatever photos we manage to take until I've shown them to you and gotten your approval. Let's be friends, Katharine. Help me, and I'll help you. Trust me, please. Now. You can leave your clothes over here and take a seat on that chair."

At this Katharine laughed out loud, and he laughed too. She shook her head – no no no – but no words came out and she found herself thinking: *Really, what the hell.* She liked this Salt despite herself. He was undeniably talented, and she had to do this. She had to do this for Nicolas. She had to find Anita. And Selena was there, setting up the camera with a look of complete seriousness. Katharine wouldn't be alone with the man, and maybe this would be a kick. After all, she finally *liked* her body again, more or less. She thought of spreading her legs for the man in that café that night, and she felt a tremor that was unmistakably sexual. So she began to unstrap her sandals as Salt moved off again. Selena had finished setting up the camera on a tripod aimed at the chair, and she went over to the high metal table, grabbed the bottle of bourbon, eyed the two glasses to determine that they were clean, then poured the glasses full and brought them over to Katharine. "To art," she said with a wink, and they both downed their shots in a flash.

Okay then. The dress was next. Katharine pulled it over her shoulders and folded it into a square. Selena stood there openly admiring her body. "*Joder!* You are bee-utiful."

"Thanks," Katharine murmured, looking around uncomfortably as Selena stared fixedly at her tits. "Now the bra," she said eagerly, and so looking off into the distance at nothing, too intimidated to meet Selena's eyes, Katharine unhooked her bra, which Selena promptly took from her hand. "Now how about the little booty," Selena cooed. Katharine had to laugh, and as her underwear came off and went into the pile, they were both giggling like lifelong girlfriends. If only Salt hadn't been there too. He was watching her so closely that he must have already taken a mental photograph of every inch of her body.

Then she had to muster the nerve to walk naked across the room to the chair in front of the camera, which was, without a doubt, the hardest thing she had ever had to do naked. It was terrifying to be watched so closely, and when she finally reached the chair and sat, she was trembling with nerves. On the chair it was better, however. Salt had begun to fiddle with the camera, which allowed her to feel like a model, not Katharine.

He worked with intense focus, snapping a few pictures, then rising from behind the tripod to fix her with his eyes and instruct her to move an arm or a leg this way or that, to hold up her hair, to stick out her tongue. "You are absolutely stunning," he murmured at one point. She found herself relaxing and beginning to enjoy the play, increasingly confident in her nudity. Selena moved around behind Salt, handing him flashes or filters, flicking on floodlights that were instantly hot on

Katharine's skin, and making approving sounds.

Occasionally Salt would come over and show her an image in the camera, and she was astonished by what she saw there. Her body was pretty fabulous, she had to admit. Those tits? Forget ballet. Those tits were worth it. And the one of her bent over the chair, and her ass? Well well. Her body was truly sexy, but what shocked her most was her face. There was lust there. She hadn't realized that she parted her lips so seductively. She had simply been trying to be a good, professional model, but in the photographs her eyes glittered naughtily, as if she was imagining orgies, the most erotic fantasies. Who was that girl? She shook these thoughts from her mind (did that look so sexy too?). She was doing this for Nicolas. She had to find Anita for Nicolas. That was all.

"Off with them," Salt said out of the corner of his mouth to Selena as he crouched at the camera again and furiously clicked. She was out her clothes in an instant – no bra, no panties – and Katharine became distracted by the spectacle. Now that was an outrageous body. Selena was like a little sports car with sleek and crazy curves. And her tits? Well, between the two of them they had some serious boobs going on in there. And also: what the hell was Selena doing taking off her clothes?

"Next to her," Salt whispered to Selena. "Ass to me." Selena hopped over to Katharine just as she'd been told. "Look at her breasts, Katharine, really look." So she did as Selena grinned back at her. "Wanna touch," Selena asked, and thrust them out even further, her dark nipples perfectly round and hard. "Your left hand across your body to her left breast," Katharine heard Salt say, and so she tentatively reached out and covered that beautiful breast with her palm. It was warm and so firm that when she gently pressed against it, it pressed right back. She felt her own nipples growing hard and looked away. "Good, Selena. Leave her now."

Selena skipped back over to him, ass bobbing attractively, and stood there beside him watching Katharine with one leg coyly crossed over the other, a hand occasionally sliding down her hip to casually brush across the dark spot between her legs. When Salt paused to study an angle or move the tripod, she would press up into him, or put a hand to his waist, her eyes glittering at Katharine.

"Kiss me," she said to him after a while, her wandering hand now firmly placed between her legs. He looked at Katharine a moment longer, then turned to Selena, cupped her ass with a big strong hand and kissed her deeply as Katharine watched. The kissing went on. Selena was openly fingering herself now, completely uninhibited, and Salt's kisses moved from her mouth to her neck to her breasts, at which he gobbled ferociously. Katharine couldn't believe her eyes, but it obviously didn't matter what she thought – Selena had found the button of Salt's jeans and was pulling them down, pulling him down onto the mattress as if the two of them were completely alone. Katharine sat there quietly – paralyzed – and she watched.

Selena was ravenous now, pulling at Salt's thighs, pulling at his underwear, as he licked at her long, hard nipples and grappled for hold on her ass. His t-shirt was off, and yes, he was a powerful man, with a wide, thick, hairy chest. He looked accustomed to rough physical labor. Selena was intent on his underwear now, ignoring his kisses to focus like a drug fiend on freeing his cock. It was hard now, swelling the cotton with dangerous promise, and after some pulling she finally freed it, bending it aside and snatching the underwear clear before it immediately popped back to attention.

Katharine had never been particularly interested in penises. She was a good American girl, filled with sweet songs and shining stars and romance, and so when she fell in love with parts of a man, it was smiles, hands, torsos, or even noses sometimes. Penises themselves weren't worth much: hard flesh put inside that either made her feel good or didn't, for reasons that sometimes escaped her. But John Salt's penis captured her attention. Perhaps the magnificent specimens in the photos he had shown her had accustomed her to look-ing. Whatever the case, she could not take her eyes from John Salt's cock. It was as big as that of the glorious black

man in the first photo she'd seen, and it was perfectly pro-
portioned with his powerful body. It was like some glorious
marble phallus, and she marveled, unable to believe what was
happening right in front of her. The penis was circumcised
in a familiar way, but totally unfamiliar – proud, enormous,
and now partly disappearing into the tiny, greedy mouth of
Selena, a sight that was disconcerting. In her life Katharine
had only taken one dick into her mouth, and it had been such
an unpleasant experience that she had spit it out and had re-
frained from sucking since, but this just looked...*delicious?*...
and she looked down across her own perfect body and knew
that the sight had made her wet, although she didn't dare test
herself with a finger.

Salt took charge. He pushed Selena off of him, and his face
dove towards the glistening patch of black hair between her
legs. The legs themselves were split in the air, bobbing slightly
to the rhythm of his tongue, which lapped at her clitoris in
slow, steady strokes. Katharine could see everything from
where she sat – Selena sucking thirstily at her own thumb and
grinding her hips up into Salt's face with little whimpers, Salt
bent over on all fours to lick like a horse at a pond, his cock
dangling between his legs. They paid Katharine no attention.
Katharine paid herself no attention, which may be why her
fingers decided on their own to test her wetness, and find it.
And her index finger, on its own, lightly traced the edge of
her swollen lips, up and down, until it found the button of

her clitoris and pressed. Then the finger was inside her, the other hand was cupping her breast as if offering it up for a suck, and she was moaning too.

Salt took Selena's knees in his hands and flipped her over with the efficiency of a wrestler. He gripped her wide hips and pulled her towards him and onto her elbows and knees, his cock hovering behind her like a weapon. He wrenched her body around until they both faced Katharine, although neither of them paid her any attention. He was rearing up into the churning gap between Selena's legs, so hard that her whole body shuddered with every thrust and her head lolled around, sweeping the mattress with her long hair. They were locked in their dreams of each other, pure lust coming off them in waves.

Katharine let herself enter the dream too. She spread her pussy with two V'd fingers and watched herself now as the fingers of her other hand circled her clitoris in quick, tight movements. Her whole body was a pussy, and everywhere she touched brought her to the edge of orgasm. She closed her eyes for a moment, which must have become more, because when she opened them Salt was still fucking Selena mercilessly from behind, but their eyes were both locked on her. She looked away, suddenly mortified at what was happening, terribly ashamed. Her cheeks flushed, and she ripped her hand from her dripping cunt, letting it hang in the air as if she didn't know what to do with it. And this was the real shame: even then she couldn't stop looking. Their eyes greedily roved her body as if they were desert wanderers spying an oasis, and she saw the final transformation coming over them, the warp into another dimension, the transfiguration into mythical beasts driving their sexes together towards one final colossal collision. They were not human now. Their bodies were slick and beautiful and well beyond the edge. In a trance, Katharine looked down at her own body, drenched with sweat, and it seemed to her that it was the most beautiful thing she had ever seen. She was not master of herself. There was some other master. She was not the one driving fingers deeply into her own cunt with a grunt. She was not the one raking her tensed belly with her nails, the one smoothing the sweat over her swollen breasts, the one with a thirst to take them in her mouth, the want who wanted to lie down and be overcome like Selena in a fuck.

Then Selena and Salt were screaming, screaming and grunting right into her dripping pussy, it seemed, and his head reared back as he drove into the slavering woman, and they were coming together, a beautiful sight, lurching through the ultimate pleasure and moaning with the joy. They were all coming, Katharine's body told her, and she began to buck uncontrollably on the chair as a strange and guttural cry went out from her mouth. Then she was shrieking and shrieking, and it was done.

Silence. Had she been asleep? She opened her eyes. She was naked, sticky, sprawled on a chair and used. Salt and Selena were drowsy on the mattress, still naked too. She managed to stand and look around the room, getting her bearings again, and then she was horrified. What had she done? With a surge of panic she ran for her dress. Her bra and panties she shoved into her purse, and the dress came over her quickly. Salt had pulled himself up to his knees to observe these activities with a satisfied smile.

"You *promised!*" she hissed at him as she hopped around on one leg trying to get a sandal attached to a foot.

"Not to touch you," he drawled. "Wouldn't dream of it, my dear. But if I'm not mistaken, you were a tad...involved."

Giving up on the sandals, she fixed him with a hatred that radiated from every pore of her body. "And Anita? *Please* tell me I didn't come here for nothing."

"You call that *nothing?*" he said as he stood, his cock dangling between his legs – that cock. "Well that's just a sacrilege, darling. And Anita? I have no idea where she is. I told you that. And if you've developed a crush and were just look-ing for more photos to tide you over, I don't have any more of those either. The one you saw is the only one I ever took worth keeping."

"You! Animal!" Katharine cried, spitting in anger. And then she was running, so furious with him, but even more, so embarrassed with herself that she didn't know what to do but run.

"Katharine! Wait! Tell me this: you're looking for a book, aren't you? A book that was stolen?"

"What?" she said incredulously, turning in confusion to face him again. He had moved from the mattress and was rummaging in another pile of junk. What was he saying? A book?

He pulled out a slim, leather-bound book and carried it towards her.

"It's a rare Kama Sutra. Don't ask questions. Take it. It's the one you're looking for."

CHAPTER THREE

She must have called Nicolas a hundred times. He wasn't picking up. She would have gone by his place a hundred times too, but she didn't know where he lived. And then, because it was Saturday morning and she was more confused than she'd even been in her life, she went back to bed. Of course she couldn't sleep. The morning was already hot, and she twisted and turned, tormented by visions of Salt's studio. At least yesterday was over. At least she had survived. Was there some pride to be taken from that? Hardly.

And now she had this book. She'd gone looking for a simple alibi, and instead she'd found the mystery. Again, hardly. The mystery was more baffling than ever. Where was Nicolas, and how was it that the one man she had visited in search of this Anita had been in possession of the book that had been stolen from her office two nights before? This Anita must be behind it all, Katharine thought, and she knew that even more than before, the woman had to be found.

She had been awake even before Michel that morning, sitting on the toilet with the rare Kama Sutra, the bathroom door locked, the shower running. There were sixty-four positions in the Kama Sutra, and the book dedicated two pages to each one: on the left page was a description of the position, and on the right was a black-and-white photograph of two lovers engaged in the position. The photographs were admittedly beautiful and in each the lovers seemed to be different, so that there were sixty-four women in the book and sixty-four men. Were the photos by John Salt? That was just one more mystery, and one she didn't feel like solving at the moment. Only this was clear: she never wanted to see Salt again.

Her first instinct the previous night as she had fled from the studio through the darkening streets of Pigalle was to return the book immediately to the office vault. By the time she was installed on the Metro for Drouot, the neighborhood where the auction houses were located, she had realized that she would not be able to enter the vault without using her own keycard, which would immediately make her the principal suspect in the theft and do Nicolas no favors either. She might find a way to slip in there unnoticed once the work week began, but again, that wouldn't help Nicolas clear his name. Monsieur Legrand would just assume he'd lost his nerve and accuse him of the crime anyway. So she couldn't return the book until she talked to Nicolas, and she couldn't talk to Nicolas until he picked up the damned phone, which she had dialed again, several dozen times since locking the bathroom door. He'd said he would be going into hiding, but this was a bit extreme.

Saturdays, even Sundays, were just another day for Michel, and now he'd gone off to work without noticing her distress. So she was back in bed, twisting and turning in a camisole top that Michel had bought for her as a replacement for the one she'd attempted to shoplift. She thought of Nicolas, she thought of the book, but more than anything she thought of Salt and Selena fucking on the mattress in front of her as she lost control and fingered herself with abandon. What kind of people did that? The images flashed through her mind: Selena's heaving breasts, her round belly, her black pubic hair, the dense muscles of Salt's butt, tensed as he stabbed forward with that cock, his silly grin, his coiled body coming towards her with the book.

Damnit! She dug her fingers into her thigh – hard – hoping to eliminate imagination with pain, but the pain just brought on new images, violent images, of her own legs spread on the mattress and John Salt standing above her. She was Selena now, and Selena was in the chair where Katharine had sat, exhibiting her masturbation with a fearlessness that was intoxicating. Defeated, Katharine took her hand from her thigh, rolled over onto her side, and reached for the vibrator in the bottom drawer. She let herself go. It was so much easier that way. She slipped the plastic nub inside of her and pressed its button, and then it was just bliss. It was facefuls of cool water and the scent of freshly cut grass. It was the man on the street to whom she'd shown her pussy, walking into the room in his sports coat. It was Selena's firm breast against her cheek, a dozen hands massaging oil into her skin in a dark room, John Salt tied to a bed, and her dancing over him with abandon. Oh, she loved her joy. She felt it ripple up her stretched legs, across the silky slip of skin between her anus and her cunt, crashing through her groin like a wave until her joy could not be contained, and she came with a girlish whimper.

But afterwards, instead of finding release, guilt returned. Why guilt? Because of Michel? She considered this for a moment, but reached the conclusion that she had in no way betrayed Michel the previous day. Maybe in her head, maybe just now again in her head, but who didn't betray their partners every day at least some way in their heads? So guilt about what? Being a "bad" girl? She laughed to herself, but the laughter quickly died, because that was it. She was guilty about having been a "bad" girl, not in the eyes of Salt or Selena, who only would have admired her more if she'd been still badder, but in the eyes of herself, or at least the Katharine who (she had to admit) she'd been trying to leave behind for a long, long time. That voice, that Katharine, was a scared girl afraid of making any wrong step, a young woman who aimed for perfection and always failed, because that's all anybody did when they aimed for perfection. She didn't want to be that Katharine anymore. She wanted to be: *open*. She wanted to adapt. Of this, at least in that moment, she was absolutely certain. Now was the time. Paris was the place she was meant to learn to take life as it came, and if that meant an embarrassing scene in the studio of John Salt, well, then she would take that too. Not repeat it, but take it. What the hell.

Feeling somewhat rejuvenated and surer of herself, she decided that she would dance for half an hour to fling the last of her doubts from her bones. She pulled on a leotard, went out to the living room, and began to stretch. Soon enough she was stepping lightly through the latest routine that Brigitte, her instructor, had been teaching them. It was a physical dance, with lots of strenuous movements down to the floor, then from the floor directly up into the air. Soon enough she was drenched with perspiration. Dance was her meditation. It didn't clear her mind entirely of thoughts, but the thoughts that did come left again easily, without rooting themselves and becoming a problem. She thought of anything and everything when she danced, easily. She thought of "good Katharine", and her childhood. She thought of Brigitte shouting out instructions. "*Vif!*" she always cried. "Make it *lively!*" Katharine and some of the girls would joke about it whenever they went out afterwards for a drink. "*Vif!*"

She muttered it under her breath now as she danced – *vif, vif, vif* – stretching herself further, pushing herself higher. She thought of Brigitte, who had danced with the Paris Opera Ballet for a few years. Although she was well into her thirties now, she was probably the most talented dancer Katharine had ever seen. She didn't have the typical dancer's body either. She was curvier, more womanly than most, as she had demonstrated to Katharine on the one evening that Katharine had stayed behind after class for a shower. Usually she just went straight back to Michel's, but on that evening she'd been meeting him out for dinner, and so she'd brought along a change of clothes.

"I'm sure you heard the speech, too," Brigitte had said as she stepped out of the shower. "I'm not quite light enough on my feet, I tend to stray from the perfect line, my breasts are too big, and whatever else they come up with to mean: *unfortunately, you're not anorexic enough for us.*" Katharine laughed and took her evening clothes from her bag. Her hair was wet, and her towel was still wrapped around her. None of the other girls ever showered at the studio, so they were alone.

"I mean look at me," Brigitte joked, casually undoing her towel to reveal her naked body. Katharine – this was the old, "good" Katharine – was suddenly uncomfortable, but she forced herself to do the polite thing and look at Brigitte's body, which was admittedly beautiful – slim and strong and beautiful. "Stupid, isn't it," Katharine said. "I mean you are *absolutely stunning.* Really."

"You mean porky little me?" Brigitte playfully asked, and shimmied like a burlesque dancer until they were both bent over in laughter. Katharine really couldn't believe what she was seeing, but this Brigitte was alright.

"And look at *you!*" Brigitte girlishly cried, and before Katharine knew what was happening, her towel had also been ripped from her body. The smile faded from Brigitte's face almost immediately. "*Putain*," she murmured. "You are fucking sexy, girl. I thought I was showing off, but you're showing off just *standing* there. Forget dancing, just *stand*, baby."

Katharine had blushed that day, of course, and had quickly recuperated her towel to cover herself again, but she laughed now even as she danced at the thought of that evening. She wondered what she would do if she found herself in the same situation now that "bad" Katharine was on the scene. It was a ridiculous thought, and it didn't matter, but she did like that Brigitte. She had spunk. She was alright.

After dancing she felt like a new woman, not "bad" or "good", but refreshed and reborn. Her mind was sharp again, her body relaxed. She decided that she would go back to the gallery that morning and see if she could get another lead on Anita from Harriet, just Harriet. Then, and only then, would she see how she felt about paying Mr. Salt another visit. She hated the idea, but it might be necessary.

First, however, it was time for a late breakfast, so she showered quickly, put on a chic blouse and short skirt in hopes of inspiring confidence in Harriet, and went down to the corner café where she stopped every morning for her croissant and *café au lait*. At the counter she put in her order, borrowed a copy of *Le Monde*, and sat down at a booth to browse the headlines and pick up some more French vocabulary. Soon enough her coffee and croissant had arrived. This was one of her favorite parts of the day, a guaranteed pleasure that never grew stale, and she positively beamed to herself as she pulled away flaky pastry to dunk into the coffee and pop into her mouth. Stylish Saturday strollers moved by on the sidewalk outside, and she felt privileged to be among them. Happiness flashed through her like sunlight through the trees. She was alive and she was glad.

Now for Harriet. Katharine had no plan, she was well off the old track, but she would just figure it out, she decided. Take it as it came. So she folded the paper back up, took a last sip of coffee, and moved to slide out of the booth. Only then did she notice that a man was blocking her exit, staring intently down at her. How long had he been standing there? She had been too lost in her reverie to notice. He was not a pleasant looking man. He wore a black tie and suit that was stretched tightly over one of the most muscular bodies she had ever seen. His hair was curly and black, he had a thick black mustache, and over his cheeks was dense, black stubble. His eyes were lit by a wildfire that could have been intelligence but looked more like plain rage.

"I got the bill," the man said in heavily accented English, without making the slightest move to let her out. "I don't know who you are, and I'll pay my own bill," Katharine huffed, and moved to push through him to the bar. The man just snickered. He wasn't going anywhere. "I feel I owe you," he said, continuing with the performance he'd clearly rehearsed. *He's seen too many movies about the mob*, Katharine thought furiously. She was accustomed to being outrageously hit upon by French men, but this guy was way out of line. "Anyway, it's already paid," the man continued, and still did not move.

"And why, exactly, do you *owe* me," she said loudly, hoping to signal her distress to the bartender. "Who *are* you?"

"A detective of sorts," he replied, reaching into his suit pocket now. Confusion clouded Katharine's face. Maybe the man had been sent by Nicolas. "And I'd lower your voice," he continued. "We don't want to draw a crowd. At least not with these on the table." With that he pulled a stack of photographs from his jacket pocket and dropped them on the table. The man had not been sent by Nicolas.

"You see now why I owe you? I've been enjoying these all morning." Katharine hardly heard him. She was staring in horror at a black-and-white image of herself, naked, sitting on a chair, her head tossed back in the throes of frantic masturbation. With a trembling hand, she swept the photos from the table and onto the seat beside her. "What does he want now," she whispered.

"Maybe we should talk someplace less…public." She nodded quickly, gathered up the photographs and moved for the narrow opening the man had cleared, her head sunk in defeat. The "detective" followed her out onto the sidewalk, where he promptly removed the photos from her hand and slipped them back into his pocket. "Your place would be best, I think," he said, almost polite. "Assuming of course that we'll be alone."

"We'll be alone," she murmured, and they walked in silence back up the street towards the apartment, Katharine numb to the world around her, including the man. Salt was behind all of this and had been since the beginning, she decided, and she also decided that she would get her revenge. Numbness was consumed by a fire for revenge.

As soon as she had shut the door of the loft behind them, the man was moving off through the rooms as if searching for intruders. He did it expertly, eyes flicking left and right, body braced whenever he came to a doorway, and Katharine wondered whether he might actually be some kind of detective. He canvassed the living room, the open kitchen (*ridiculous*, she thought), then the bathroom, and finally the bedroom. And then he didn't appear again. Katharine swallowed hard, unstuck herself from the floor, and followed. As she came through the bedroom door, he slowly turned to look at her and said: "I think I've found a bug."

"*What?*" she cried, her voice strangled by terror. Then he held out his hand. In it was her vibrator, which she must have left out that morning. On the bed, she saw in the same glance, were the dozen naked photographs of her, fanned out like playing cards. He grinned: "All very exciting, *n'est-ce pas?* I like a woman who knows what she wants. Pick a card?"

"Who are you?" Katharine hissed, her hands clenched into fists. Obviously he found this amusing. He was in control here. A man built like that was always in control, here and everywhere. He moved towards her with the vibrator still in his palm. She resolved not to budge. This was her house (*Michel's house*, said a voice inside), and she would not be threatened or intimidated. She stood her ground as the man came closer and closer, her fists clenched so tightly now that they ached.

"I'm on your side," the man said softly, and with one quick motion he flicked on the vibrator and reached down to place it against the inside of her thigh. His eyes never left hers as he did this. She held them, her mouth twisted into a grimace, her body refusing to move, even as the man gradually slid his vibrating palm higher and higher. *This is my house! He has no right!* The vibrator was cold, and she shivered. That vibrating cold was the only sensation she felt now. The sensation was beginning to make her dizzy, beginning to make her feel as if she was melting around the edges, although it was cold, and her dumb, brute, Pavlovian response to the apparatus infuriated her. Was that desire rising up inside? It didn't matter. If it was desire she would channel it into rage, and in that moment rage overtook her and her fists were up, and she was pummeling this stranger who had walked into her house and taken such liberties. She hit and she hit. It was like punching a block of concrete.

He let her rage on, and even her most violent thrusts did not budge him an inch. Now he held the vibrator tightly against the dimple in her underwear, but she hardly felt it. The ripple that had begun in her groin was lost in the overwhelming surge of emotion that had overtaken her body. She wanted to pound him until he disappeared, and she disappeared too, but when his face lowered gently to hers, oblivious to the spasm of rage that she was unleashing upon him, she found herself kissing him back with all the violence in her heart. Her arms dropped limply to her sides, and then it was just a normal kiss for a moment longer, until she caught herself and lurched away. "No!" she snarled.

"Let me in," he said coolly. "Let me in and you can take those photos off my hands."

She stared broodingly at the floor. She had no idea what

would happen next or what she would say. It turned out to be this: "No. At least not in here."

In Michel's room. In their room.

So she turned, eyes still cast to the floor, and walked out into the living room. She felt the man close behind her, a terrifying force that seemed negligible compared to the force of the conflicting emotions that had overwhelmed her. She came to the couch, and she felt his arms around her waist, and her neck could no longer support her head, and she slumped into his arms as he covered her face with kisses. So let him strip her naked, let him have his way. She just couldn't think anymore, so let him rake her blouse from her chest, and let him plunge her skirt to her heels as if it was a mob adversary he was intent on drowning. Let him shove his hand down the front of her panties, and let him find her wet and wanting. Her bra was already off, after all, her breasts unloosed for him to find with his mouth, and for her to feel his stubble scraping across their pristine skin as he flicked his tongue across nipples.

Yes, his suit jacket was off, his shirt too, and yes, she would admit that the sight of his hulking shoulders made her want to wrap her arms around them, at least right then in that crazy moment. "Just fuck me," she said dully, and then it was she who was fumbling with his belt and sending his pants cascading to the floor. But he was the one who fished his dick from his pants and wielded it like a baton, and he was the one who pulled her from the top of the couch and pushed her head down until it was at the level of his sex.

"Show me how you suck," he said, but she gritted her teeth and shook her head. She took the cock in both hands, suddenly feeling like a little girl, dwarfed by his size, and still shaking her head, trance-like, she said: "No. I won't do that. That's what I won't do."

He was gentler with her than she had expected. He did not force his bulging sex upon her lips. Instead, with her eyes still fixed upon that fascinating danger, and those impossible thighs, as thick and as solid as tree trunks, he pulled her up and into him and kissed her mouth deeply, his tongue probing past her teeth until she had no choice but to force him back with her own hot tongue and kiss. As she did, she felt herself being lightly lifted up, and she wrapped her legs around his waist, giving over entirely. She felt herself glide weightlessly through the air, his hands spreading her ass, his pinky tantalizing the pinched entrance of her anus.

Then he set her down on the back edge of the couch. With her locked legs around his waist as her only support, she arched her spine and tossed back her head, wanting to go dizzy, or to conquer the vertigo. Behind her she saw for a moment the upside-down world outside. Then she tensed the muscles of her stomach and arched back up into him, wrapping her arms tightly around the thick cords of his neck for another kiss. It was a dance, that was all. Pure movement that she couldn't begin to explain.

"So do it," she said through a kiss, and his body was tight on hers so quickly that she gasped. They fit like pieces of a puzzle, and his cock inside, as thrilling as it was, was no more thrilling than every other inch of his capable body notched perfectly into hers. She tensed her ass and extended her legs straight out to the sides with her toes pointed in order to make a line of herself and get even closer to him – the scratch of the hair on his chest and belly, the blocks of his arms, his sweet, dank scent. He fucked her like that for a while, and she let herself go all the way because there was no place else to go.

When he pulled out, she gasped again, but this time it was as if a bucket of cold water had been dumped on her head, and the anger that she had swallowed surfaced again, and she beat at his chest with a fury, eyes shooting fire. No thoughts could anchor themselves in her mind in this storm of emotions. Emotions were demons, and dozens of them had overtaken her. She was flesh and bone animated only by sensations, which shot through her like electrical currents. Never had she ever felt more primitive, or more destroyed, or more herself.

"Like this now," the man growled, placidly submitting to

her blows in order to sweep her legs out around him and up above his head. "Straight as swords," he grunted. "Keep them that way."

Her legs shot up straight in front of her now, locked into place on his shoulders with her feet above her head, toes still pointed in some mad ballet. She began to fall backwards onto the couch, but the man placed both hands on the small of her back and pulled her towards him as his cock simultaneously reentered the tensed and shining crevasse that protruded now from the backs of her thighs. He pulled her body into a tight V as he entered her more deeply than she had ever felt anyone inside, and a grunt escaped her mouth from some dark corner of herself. She was tense at first, straining to hold a position that only a dancer could have held, feeling the pull in her hips and at the backs of her thighs, but soon she was drawn more to the pleasure and discovered that she could relax completely. The man's shoulders kept her legs extended, and his hands kept her back straight and her body folded in two. She let her head fall back and let herself be handled. She even let herself smile a crooked smile. She was nothing but a pussy. That was all she could feel, and this was without a doubt the most delicious position ever devised by the sex gods. It was as if she could feel every little millimeter of him, every swell of every vein in his cock, every curve of its blood-tight head, sliding on and on, in and out, over every millimeter of the tight and throbbing walls of a pussy that was discovering a new and thrilling possibility.

Vibrators were easy, but she rarely came with a man on intercourse alone. She needed to be licked and prodded with attention before she could explode. With the detective, however, she felt it coming in just minutes, and because she felt him so precisely too, she knew that he was as close as she was. God, she just *felt* him so well, but then her brain clicked back on and she had a hand on his belly and was edging him out her. She looked into his face, which was still just as fearsome, but also vulnerable now in its own lust daze, and she said: "Not in me. On me."

He obeyed. She had that power at least. He let her draw him out until the lips of her pussy closed over his freed head, which had turned a livid red. As soon as they separated, he was hitching back up towards her, the vein sharply lining the base of his cock sliding up through the lips of her pussy, over her clitoris, and into the twist of pale hair through which she now raked her nails. Up and down, he split her without penetrating her, and she made her fingers into a V that echoed the V of her body and stroked the edge of her lips, feeling the length of his cock move over her knuckles like a train on rails. Her muscles were loose now and made no resistance as she bent even further forward to watch this new technique, her chin almost touching her knees. She was enthralled. It was one of the most incredible sights she had ever seen, and it was her pussy, and it was this brute of a man. The sight did her in. He was entranced by the same sight as she, and it must have done him in too. She was coming like a bomb with just her two fingers pressing down across her lips and his blunt cock moving through just the edge of her wetness like a boat over the surface of a lake. She ratcheted her torso even further forward, straining towards the feeling until her knees were at her ears and she screamed. Her scream exploded simultaneously with the man, who pressed the base of his cock and his balls against her clitoris, with the head standing clear in the air, to shoot lashes of hot come up over her belly and tits.

Then he collapsed away from her, and her feet plummeted to smack the floor, and she was standing there dazed as the man stumbled blindly around the living room as if he had just extricated himself from a car crash. She looked down at her body, which was covered with his slick, white semen. The liquid went clear when she smoothed it over her nipples. She played with herself like an innocent discovering sex for the first time, and she marveled.

And then she wanted him out. Thankfully he seemed to feel the same way. He was already dressing himself, grunting at an uncooperative zipper. He would not meet her eyes, even as he slid the knot of his tie back into place and took one last glance around the room to make sure he hadn't forgotten anything. Then he nodded vaguely in her direction and shuffled towards the door, slamming it shut behind him. Still dazed, she stood there for a minute or two longer before she realized that he'd taken the photos with him. That had been the deal, and he'd betrayed her. The anger was there again, burning in her gut, but for the moment, at least, she was tired of emotions. That had been the deal? Who the hell knew what the deal really was in all of this insanity? She slowly walked into the kitchen, cleaned herself with a towel hung over the oven door, then wandered around some more, lost in her own apartment.

Michel arrived home later that evening. She was reading in bed, wearing her Katharine mask and stuck on the same page. He'd closed a deal, or won a case, or something, and she let him fuck her. She knew she reeked of the other man, but Michel didn't notice. She was falling apart, but Michel didn't notice. So stick your dick in my pussy and get your pleasure, man. I just fucked an animal. I just let a beast come all over me, and I didn't mind. Hell, I *liked* it, boyfriend, and you know what else (she realized this as she thought it): I didn't even get his name. *Shut your mouth,* she thought to her inner voice. *Don't be cruel.*

Michel reached orgasm in a few dozen precise strokes, and as he did she moaned louder than she ever had before. She felt nothing from him, but strangely enough, there was pleasure in the moaning. She was "bad" Katharine now, Katharine long gone, and she was moaning for the ears of other men. Did she hate herself for this? Yes, but she also loved herself for it. She was not a bad girl at heart, she knew, and for once in her life she felt *formidable*.

After Michel had crashed off to sleep, she found that she had finally shaken off her torpor. She crept out of bed to find the book again, which she had hid behind the others on his bookshelves. Michel had once been a reader, the brightest at his university, but now his bookshelf was just an indication to handpicked guests that he had once been a reader, the brightest at his university. The only person who touched them now was Fatima the maid, to whom he had given explicit instructions for their dusting.

She didn't bother to smuggle the book into the bathroom. Michel had enjoyed his love moment with her and wouldn't stir till morning. She flipped through the pages, studying the bodies bent into strange poses and looking for answers for which she didn't even know the questions. It took her a while to find it, on her second or third skim through.

It went like this: first, she noticed that the pages were strangely numbered. They started with 100, and then occasionally they would skip a few dozen numbers, so that a book with 128 pages ended up on page 311. Pressing her fingers into the valley between pages, however, she could find no sign that any of them were missing; second, the photographs were more detailed than she had first noticed. Yes, there were these fabulous bodies doing fabulous things (had the nameless detective made her so blasé?), but there were also more details if you looked closely – another face in a mirror, a poster for an Italian opera, and in every single photograph, at least a word or two, whether a headline in a magazine, a sign out an open window, or something nearly inscrutable scrawled across a chalkboard; third, page 182, a blonde shorter and skinnier than Katharine was seated on a wooden table with her legs straight up in the air and held to her chest as an indistinct man fucked her. It was the exact same position in which the detective had fucked Katharine – the position that he had *insisted* upon – and she couldn't help but think that she was about to discover one of her answers. The position was called the White Lily. *Okay,* she thought ruefully. *So I've mastered the White Lily. Now what.*

She studied the photograph closely. It looked as if it had been staged in a church or a chapel. At least that's how it seemed to Katharine. The table itself looked heavy and ecclesiastical, and in the background was a gaudily lit altar of the sort you see in Italy or South America, littered with flowers and icons and little oddball offerings. There was a small painting of a haloed saint in the center of the altar and over his head in an ornate script were the words, just discernible: *Saint Martin.*

182. Saint Martin. Okay, she flipped to another page. 111.

Invalides (a bit of a sign on what was presumably a hospital in the background). Yes, she was tired and desperate and probably losing her mind, but could they be…street numbers? She ran for the bookshelf and found an atlas, then brought both it and the Kama Sutra to the dining table in order to give herself more room to work. Working the atlas with her left hand and the Kama Sutra with her right, she went through the pages one by one, and with every page she felt a growing confidence that she might not be so crazy after all. Every number and word combination could potentially correspond to a Paris address. Once she had gone through the entire book, she slumped back into her chair, exhausted now but satisfied. Was that an answer?

CHAPTER FOUR

Sunday mornings are the guiltiest ones. If you've slept with (*slept* with? hardly) a man who's not your boyfriend, and you've done it in your boyfriend's living room in spectacular fashion, you'll awake early (if afterwards you haven't had too much to drink) and you'll start thinking about reform. You'll hate the nostalgia you feel for a time when Sunday mornings were so innocent and free, and you'll desperately wonder what you might do to capture that feeling again. You'll take a long, hot shower and scrape your entire body with a pumice stone, trying to eliminate the scent of the nameless man. You'll wash your hair twice, digging your nails into your scalp. And when your boyfriend calls out something through the locked door, you'll pretend you didn't hear. The shower will make you feel clean. Scrub yourself inside and out, and it may even make you feel like a girlfriend again. It may make you want to throw your arms around him, treat him like a sweetheart, and rededicate yourself with those words you've as yet found it impossible to say to the man: *I love you.*

That Sunday morning, at least, it worked. She emerged from the bathroom pink and dry and even a little horny, believe it or not, at least in a girlfriend sort of way. She would surprise him wherever he was, probably in front of the computer at the bedroom desk, and cover his body with kisses. Was it possible that she was *happy*, and that the unwise insanity of yesterday didn't matter so much at all? Dancing out into the living room, feeling like a fairy or a sprite (whatever that was), she leapt and leapt and leapt – *tout nu* – across the room in front of the windows, then leapt and leapt and leapt again, back towards the bedroom with her arms tossed in the air. *Vif! Vif!*

A quick little delicious tickle of the pussy, and then *vif!*, she chorus line kicked into the bedroom. And Michel wasn't there. "Michel?" she called out. Michel wasn't anywhere.

She felt as if she'd been slapped, but underneath the disappointment and the exasperation was a creeping worm of fear. She had refused to think about the very real danger in which she might now be, with strange men out there willing to rape her and nude photos circulating for the next blackmailer to use, and suddenly she just knew that Michel had been kidnapped or hurt, and that it was all her fault. She ran for her phone on the kitchen counter. There was a message. She clicked it, and it was from Michel. "Working till dinner," it said, "then let's do something nice." She snapped the phone shut. Then she watched her arm swing back and hurl it across the room.

Sunday mornings were different now. She wasn't a child anymore, and she had to learn to embrace the complications. And that man the day before? She was *glad* she had fucked him. She had *liked* it, and you know what else? She was *glad* she hadn't gotten his name. Who cared. And those photographs? Let him have them, let him enjoy them. When he'd walked into her house against her will, he'd had the power, but she had the power now. And finally: Michel? Let him work. Let him keep dotting his i's and crossing his t's without having any idea at all what the words themselves meant. Let him just stay clueless, okay?

Not that she would go looking for trouble today. Nicolas' mystery was getting out of hand, and it was time for her to get serious and get to the bottom of this thing. She put on her most conservative dress, which covered her shoulders and knees. She would be a detective of her own now. This wouldn't be a childhood Sunday morning, but a college Sunday morning: hours spent in the library getting things done. She would find Anita and get the book back to Nicolas. Today.

First step: call Nicolas, and he will sense the force of your will and swiftly pick up the phone. Revised first step: on your hands and knees, find the tossed telephone beneath the couch on which you discovered new positions, and on which there may well now be a suspicious stain. Actual first step: call Nicolas. Of course he doesn't pick up. So next step: 182 Rue Saint-Martin.

It was a longshot, she knew, and as hard as she tried to believe that she would make an efficient little detective, there was a significant part of her that doubted her own sanity. Believing that a book was communicating to her in secret codes was almost as certifiably loony as masturbating to a couple fucking across the room from her, or bringing an unknown man into her home and letting him twist her body around so that she would later decide that this had been not just a fuck, but a Very Important Message. She almost told the taxi driver to turn around. Lovers were tossing Frisbees in the Jardin de Tuileries, and she wished that she could be there with them, sporting in the sunshine. Then she had to admit with a smile that tossing Frisbees was one of the most ridiculous pastimes ever devised by mankind and that even on a good day she wouldn't be caught dead with, or even near, one. It wouldn't hurt to check out 182 Rue Saint-Martin. Worst-case scenario, she would realize that she had read too much into the book, and into the nameless detective, and she would walk down to the Centre Pompidou nearby to look at the art. It was Sunday, after all.

She climbed out of the taxi in front of an apartment building. So this was it, she thought as she stepped over to the doorway, doubting herself more with each passing second. The door was locked, but there was a buzzer next to it with a dozen names to press. There were the Blancs, the Delons, and the Duchamps. No Lenoirs or Salts, she couldn't help but notice. Also there was a fine establishment that called itself Hosnani

Consulting on the second floor. What the hell was she doing?

She decided to start with the Blancs and tentatively pressed the button. Sweet Grandmother Blanc would open the door and faint to the floor when Katharine revealed that she had the great pleasure of paying a visit that day because a man had fucked her with her legs shot up in the air, and she'd consequently cracked the code. Alas, no voice crackled through the speaker in response to her buzzing. So the Delons. They weren't home either. The Duchamps? Out throwing Frisbees, possibly with the Frappiers or the Orcels, who were also silent. That left Hosnani Consulting as a last option, and although she seriously doubted that anyone did any consulting on a Sunday, she rang the buzzer while plotting her path down to the museum. The door clicked open immediately.

Walking slowly up the stairway, she had to stop to catch her breath. She was in perfect shape but was huffing as if she'd climbed two dozen stories. It was fear, she knew. Even if someone appeared at the door and let her in, she had no idea what to say. She hadn't thought this through. She had gotten ahead of herself again, and she thought back to her shower that morning as if that was the present tense and that was where she was meant to be. Nevermind. If this was indeed where she was meant to be, then surely the people of Hosnani Consulting would let her know. There was a gold plaque on the door, more elegant than she had expected, and she rang the buzzer. For a moment there was no sound, and then a knob turned and the door was opened.

Hosnani Consulting was a pleasant surprise, the first being the woman who appeared in the doorway. Her skin was a deep, smooth black, her long hair was swept up off her neck and held into place with a stylish gold clasp, and her dark green suit, which she wore buttoned over nothing, was perfect and feminine and cut short over about five miles of legs. She made Katharine feel petite, particularly when she looked down on her with a haughty stare and said: "Yes?"

For a moment Katharine was unable to respond. She had never seen a more beautiful woman. Her cheekbones – they were as high and haughty as her voice. She looked as if she was just a few years out of a career as that exotic and feline supermodel from Africa whom every hot designer is mad about. She was another species entirely.

Was this Mrs. Hosnani? Should she ask for Hosnani, whoever he or she was? Before Katharine could decide on an approach, the woman was waving her into an office and inviting her to have a seat. "Would you like some coffee?" she asked, to which Katharine nodded a bit too emphatically. No other words were exchanged. The woman walked across the room in criss-crossing heels to an expensive-looking machine and fed it a capsule. Katharine nervously looked around the room, which was as stylish as the woman. An enormous Persian carpet covered the floor, the furniture was modern and original, and on the walls there were stone Egyptian reliefs that to Katharine's eye looked priceless. "Listen," she said out to the room. "It's a Sunday. I don't even know if I'm in the right place. I apologize if…I mean…"

"Mister Hosnani is just finishing up some business," the woman purred, turning to bring a porcelain espresso cup on its porcelain saucer over to the glass table in front of Katharine's chair, so gracefully that it was as if every slight movement had been consciously designed as its own work of art. Then she returned to an inlaid desk, sat at a wide wooden chair carved like a throne, and began to type like a concert pianist at a keyboard. Bewildered, Katharine looked at the coffee on the table and wondered whether she should drink it. One sip, and she'd be tied up in the trunk of a sedan.

God, she hated this. So she reached out and knocked back the whole cup. It was good coffee. Of course it was good coffee. So exceptionally, unusually delicious that for the first time she figured she might just be in the right place.

The office was air-conditioned, and Katharine shivered even in her modest dress. The woman appeared to have forgotten about her completely. Minutes passed. She clutched her purse to her hip. It was bulky with the shape of the book, which she had brought in case she needed visual aids. Now that just seemed like folly. How would she ever begin to explain? She could only hope that Hosnani would explain it to her. And if she was in the wrong place, well, then at least she would know. At least then she could forget about the book and concentrate only on Anita.

Finally a buzzer sounded and the secretary rose from her chair as if she'd been expecting it at that precise instant. She nodded to Katharine, her face illuminated by a beguiling smile. The woman was so…*pleasant*. Katharine stood, head spinning, and wondered again if something had been slipped into her coffee. Then a man was standing in the doorway, and he was so pleasant too.

"Nessim Hosnani," he said sharply as he extended a hand. She trembled as she took it and said her name (saying his name again inside: *Nessim Hosnani*). "Please call me Nessim," she heard him say. Okay Nessim. What a beautiful man: an inch or two taller than she, olive skin, olive eyes, priceless suit, full lips, shaved head. In the movies he would have played a principled Arab playboy or the head of a well-financed Middle Eastern intelligence agency. He led her into his office, crisply thanking the woman (who was apparently called Neema) and shut the door behind them. Then there was even more of Mr. Hosnani to discover.

His art. It was breathtaking. He saw her jaw drop and smiled with genuine pleasure. "Are you a connoisseur of Ancient Egyptian art," he asked (could a voice be called "olive" too?).

"Early twentieth-century Europeans, actually," she stammered, "but these are just amazing." On tables around the spacious, well-lit room, as well as across the walls, were Ancient Egyptian reliefs, statues, busts and pylons.

"Let me take you on a little tour," he said indulgently, and then he patiently took her from one piece to the next, explaining each one: a relief from the tomb of Khereuf, eighteenth dynasty; a bust of Ankh-haf found at Giza; an archaistic diorite statue from the thirtieth dynasty (even she didn't know what that meant, exactly). As they traversed the room, she clumsily filled the silences he left for contemplation to yammer about her own work in the art world, her studies at Columbia, her love for the Futurists. He gallantly praised her autobiography, seeming politely amused, but she hardly noticed, as enraptured as she was by this elegant man and his astonishing art. Finally he invited her to have a seat at his desk. Overcome with sensations, she did so with relief. He glided around the desk to sit and face her, and then he just stared with those glittering, olive eyes, not saying a word. The purse in her lap felt as if it was filled with bricks, or evidence of a crime that she'd stubbornly kept. Was she meant to say something now?

She looked up into his eyes, but couldn't take that for too long and looked back down at her purse. Alright. She had to say something, and whatever she said it could hardly sound more foolish than the way she already looked: "Thank you for seeing me," she murmured to her purse. "And I may be making a terrible mistake...*please* forgive me if I am...but I thought you might be able to help me...Nessim?" Shyly, she glanced up at him again to see how this had gone. He still had that same bemused look on his face.

"It would be my pleasure," he said (maybe the voice was more like olive *oil*, wonderfully golden and delicious). "We handle all sorts of situations for our clients. We invest in companies for them. We also invest in people for them. How can I help you?"

"What does that mean?" she asked darkly.

"Nothing mysterious," he said with a smile. "We create connections. We open doors. We arrange advantageous situations."

"You know," she said, mustering some American pluck and smiling at him brightly. "Consulting has been a mystery to me for years, and I can't say you've cleared up the mystery."

He laughed, then stared straight through to her palpitating heart. Now the office didn't seem nearly cold enough, but she summoned the last of her pluck to try a different tack: "My boss is...missing. He needs help, or I need help in finding him, and I was told that with your *connections*, you might be able to…guide me."

There was a long pause during which the benevolent expression on his face didn't move a millimeter, and then he purred: "Who sent you?"

She couldn't trust him yet with her story, and so she met his stare and said: "I can't say."

"Well," he said, turning his hand through the air like an emperor signaling for the death of a gladiator.

"Wait!" she cried, and his hand fell to the desk. "There's also a woman. Anita is her name, actually, and she's mixed up in all of this. Very beautiful, a model I think. She sometimes poses for an American artist named John Salt. Dark, curly hair? Exotic looking, maybe Latin? Very…curvy? Do you…?"

"I believe I do know this Anita," he said simply, still waiting for more.

"Is she maybe a *client?*" Katharine stammered on.

"I'm afraid I don't talk about my clients," he said, and then with emphasis: "Whether she's a client or not." He began to rise. "Very well. Then let me give you my card in case you reach some kind of clarity about your situation. In any case, it's always a pleasure to show off my collection to a knowledgeable and beautiful woman. Here, before you go...." He winked and waved her over to a cabinet against the wall beside the desk. "I'll show you something special."

Clutching her bag to her stomach, she walked over to stand beside him. He opened the cabinet doors. Inside it was filled with drawers of different sizes and shapes. He pulled out a wide, flat one and beckoned to her again. She came closer until her arm brushed against his and they were looking down into the drawer together. She had never seen a drawer like that.

With any other man she might have been afraid, but with Nessim, in his dazzling office, with his glorious art on the walls, she just marveled.

"Are they Egyptian," she whispered, letting her purse slide to the floor, her body tingling all over.

"Yes. Not ancient, though. Early twentieth-century to the best of my knowledge. I found them in a shop in Alexandria. They were in a back room full of priceless objects the dealer rarely showed, in a specially made drawer. I had this cabinet made for them. They're ebony. Go ahead. Hold one."

And so she reached into the drawer and drew out a cylinder of meticulously carved ebony. Some would have called it a dildo, but the word seemed too silly for such a beautiful thing. There were eleven in the drawer, each one set into its own nest of molded felt. Each had been carved with veins so lifelike that they seemed to throb before her eyes, and each except the thinnest one swelled with masterful craftsmanship to the pointed dual lobes of a head that looked as real as a petrified man's. Entranced, Katharine pored over the drawer's contents. There were chubby ones, long ones, pricks in all their infinite variety. One was only as big around as her pinky, but long – she had no idea how it might be used. Then there was a trio of phalluses carved similarly, differing only in length. And then one massive piece that seemed to gleam as if it were alive. It was a gross caricature of a penis, a full twelve inches long and thick as a woman's forearm. The sight terrified her, but already she felt the itch to contain one. Ever since she'd leapt from the shower that morning, on this strangest of all weekends, she had felt sexually thwarted (she now realized). And now here were these glorious ebony cocks.

She reached for the largest one. It struck terror into her as she drew it from the box. Even handling the monstrous thing was an experience, and she winced as she tried to imagine it pressing into her vagina, which was throbbing now with a growing need.

"Choose another one," Nessim suggested, and she hesitated for a moment. Then, like a puppet attached to strings, she replaced the heavy tool and chose another that was about eight inches long. Her hand could not quite circle it around, and she thought dumbly: *That's about the size of John Salt's cock.* She ran a finger down the piece in admiration. "Wonderful choice," Nessim said, in the tone that waiters used when Michel selected wine, but then Michel didn't matter anymore because he could not give her this.

"And what's the thinnest one?" she asked breathlessly.

"The anus," he said, his cheek close to hers as he watched her touch the one in her hand. "Some swear by it. Some will use it to enhance a bigger one."

"One in...*both?*" she gasped. He nodded and put his hand over hers to gently take the dildo. "And the biggest one?" she asked, reaching to keep her hand against his. "How could anyone ever?"

"We won't start there," he said with a smile, "but you'd be surprised. Women's bodies adapt quickly, and I am told that it is one of the most exquisite sensations in the world." With this he unhooked the case from the drawer and carried it over to the desk, where he set it down. "Come here."

She did as she was told. She was entranced by this ebony sex and wanted to know and feel more.

"Let me show you," he said, turning towards her, charming man. As nervous as she was, she did not hesitate. No, finally, she knew that she had come to the right place. She was moving deeper into the mystery, just as she had set out to do, and it was much greater than Nicolas Lenoir. The mystery was her too, and all of the indescribable pleasures her body might feel but had never been allowed to feel before. She would follow Nessim Hosnani anywhere, because she trusted him, because he was beautiful, and because he was leading them towards her undiscovered pleasure, which was a place Katharine knew she must find.

Holding the dildo lightly, Nessim moved around behind her until his smooth chin brushed gently against her cheek. She felt his hand at her thighs, pulling her skirt up towards her waist. As if following a script that had already been written, she put her hands on the desk and leaned forward as the skirt came all the way up over her innocent white panties. She let him look. She shifted her legs back and forth, moving her ass against his hand, which held the beautiful antique piece. He calmly slid the ebony across the white cotton, sending a thrill up her spine as it passed her anus, then down between her legs. She spread these ever so slightly, and then he went further, edging it up and over the moistening patch of material beneath her pussy, back and forth, sliding more slowly now because of her dampness. He stroked until she could hardly stand it anymore and murmured: "Please Nessim, take them off."

With his free hand he pulled the underwear down to her thighs, and she shivered at the feel of the material slipping slowly down her legs. "I didn't know if I'd come to the right place," she sighed.

"Did you really think I'd be consulting on a Sunday?" he joked. It was the first offhand remark he had made since they'd met, and she burst out laughing, a laughter that was cut short when the dildo tapped against her pussy again, this time unobstructed by cotton. She bent her head until the top of it touched the desk and watched as he slowly, carefully, brought the flared head of the instrument to the pink squiggle of her labia, then thrust it forward so that her lips spread to swallow the hard girth. He let it rest there for a moment, until she flipped her hair back over her shoulder to look around at his dazzled expression. The sight of her spread cunt transfixed him, she could see, and licking her lips she pressed back further against his hand and shyly said: "Give me more."

Nessim obeyed. Grasping the instrument firmly now, he slid the length of it into Katharine's slickening sheath – and again, and again – as the room's silent hum was shattered by her moans of pleasure. "God it's big!" she cried. "Drive it into me! Don't stop!" And now she felt his thumb at her anus, pressing gently there as he repeatedly sunk the prick inside her with his fingers. She felt his hot breath at her neck, and then fingers at her left nipple, pinching it in time with the deepening strokes. The sensation softened Katharine's cries into a whimper of pure bliss. Then, suddenly, Nessim whipped the prick out of her cunt, trailing transparent strands of her juices.

"Don't stop now," she cried passionately. "I'm begging you!"

"Let's try something else," he said, reaching for the tray of dildos to exchange the first for a somewhat larger second. "Climb up on the desk. I want you on all fours so that I can show you something." She turned to face him with gleaming eyes and heaving chest, then carelessly unfastened the buttons down the front of her dress before ripping it from her shoulders. Her bra came off just as quickly, freeing her breasts in an elastic bounce before it was tossed off to floor. She irritably kicked her underwear from her ankles and gamely hopped her ass up onto the cool desk. Then her legs were up and swinging around. Her heels flashed by like daggers. She put her palms to the desk and twisted around until she was on her hands and knees, sweeping a pile of paperwork aside. She posed there for a moment as Nessim stared reverently. "You are a masterpiece," he said, running the back of his fingers along her spine as if petting a mythical unicorn. She was just thinking about the next dildo, however, the itch inside having become even more maddening. Then, deciding her ass needed a better angle, she dropped from her hands to her elbows and stuck it out seductively.

With his forearm resting on her ass, he calmly inserted the

fresh object. Her cunt swallowed it greedily this time, and she quickly sat back until she contained the length of it. He began to move it in and out, as precisely as a doctor performing surgery, and she bucked and bucked, loving the smooth feel of it against her vagina walls. Soon enough she couldn't resist the urge to join her hand to his and add five fingers to her delight, and she reached back for her clitoris. She wrapped fingers around the ebony to feel it move, and soon it was wrapped tightly in her hand as Nessim relinquished his grip and stepped away to watch her self-contained fuck. God, she loved him looking at her like that. She moved the dildo faster and faster but became distracted when she saw him moving for the tray again. This time he had taken up the largest one, the terrifying one, and was weighing it in his palm.

"I can't!" she cried, staying her hand.

"It shouldn't hurt now," he whispered reassuringly. "I promise it won't." With this he took a sort of disk that had been hidden beneath the monstrous dildo and placed it on the desk between her legs. Then he set the ebony cylinder inside the disk so that it pointed straight up towards her dank and dripping pussy. The rounded end of its oversized head was just an inch or two from her swampy entrance, from which Nessim now gently pulled the second dildo before stepping back to observe her with the third. Katharine watched this happen with her head on the desk and now looked down the length of her body to the dark spike that she was somehow meant to join. She was terrified, but she could not take her eyes away from it. "It will split me!"

But lust had obliterated all resistance, and she found herself obeying the soothing commands of Nessim. Consumed by the spell of him and this overpowering lust, she spread her thighs, spread her sopping lips with her fingers, and haltingly lowered herself onto the tip of its enormity as Nessim coolly watched.

"Are you paying attention?" she heard him say. "Are you seeing yourself? You are exquisite, Katharine. Take it as deeply as you wish."

Gritting her teeth she slowly forced the head to fill her opening. Particle by particle she slowly forced it in, urged on by the reverent Nessim. She felt its massive tip disappear into her vagina, and the searing pain she had anticipated did not come. Quivering in delight, tears of fearful joy streamed down her face. "It's inside!" she gasped, her hips beginning to gently roll against the construction. And in her madness, in that searing joy, a stream of profanity shot from her lips unlike anything she had ever said or thought before. "Fuck me, Nessim!" she roared, laughing and crying. "Put your cock inside me now. Give it to me! *Bite me*, Nessim! Put your thumb in my anus and come on my face! Fuckfuckfuckfuckfuck! It's impaling me!"

Her hot words finally overcame his cool. He moved until he

was standing beside her face, and she shifted her weight onto one arm so that she could paw at his swelling groin. Slipping up and down on the dildo with tight, controlled movements, hot waves of pleasure washed over her body. Nessim had his zipper down now as she nodded blindly, and he was pulling out a cock as hard and as smooth as the ones she had put inside her. It was just as beautiful and almost as dark, but it hypnotized her even more than the others had, at least until he stepped closer and she saw what she was meant to do. "I…I don't do that," she said in a whisper. The waves of pleasure washed out of her, and suddenly the impossible width of the piece inside her was uncomfortable. Nessim nodded sharply and folded his cock back into his pants.

Tears streamed down her face. She couldn't bear the thought of lacking him, and her lust surmounted another fear as she reached out for his cock again with a desire impossibly amplified. It slipped out of his pants easily, eager for her mouth. It was the smell, or the taste, or just the gagging that she had always feared, but as the alluring red pulp of her lips covered the pulsing tip of his living member, she was intoxicated. He was delicious, and she was making him moan. She licked the tip, then licked its length, flicking briefly at his balls, which made the whole piece leap excitedly. Her lips went around it again, a quick suck and then a deeper taste. She could take him much deeper than she had ever expected a man could be taken in a mouth, and she could lick him that way too, smothering his base vein with the captured flat of her tongue. She drew back for a moment to look at the beautiful, glistening thing. Out of the corner of her eye she caught sight of the black spike still inside of her, and she saw that on their own accord her hips were grinding more deeply down onto it now. The sight of those two cocks arrayed so perfectly for her sole pleasure nearly drove her over the edge of orgasm, but she managed to hold on for more.

She was hungry at Nessim's cock now, sucking deep, lifting with her slavering tongue the salty bead of excitement that had formed at the eye atop the head. God, she wanted him to fuck her, and god, she never wanted the monstrous ebony to leave her either. She made a pussy of her mouth and fucked him that way, manically bobbing along his length as her hair fell into her face, taking him so deeply that she could feel the cold, rough zipper of his pants against her lips. She tasted more of him now, he was close to an explosion, and the horror she had always felt at the prospect of receiving such a gush had vanished entirely. She traced a line up the base of it again, then covered it with her mouth again, lips puckered as if in a kiss. And then he was coming, great lashes of salty, silver juice, and she was determined to take it all in. Delicious wasn't the word. It was an acquired taste, but she acquired it in an instant. It was salty and milky and even made her wince, but then Nessim was moaning, trembling himself now with violent pleasure, and the dildo was splitting her further, and she had done it, she had crossed the border – and all those elements combined made the taste one of the most delicious ones she had ever known.

She swallowed, and then she laughed, overcome with joy, and the joy shifted to make her cunt the center of her world again, and almost instantly she felt the onrushing torment of a shattering orgasm. Nessim brushed her hair from her sweat-drenched face as she thrashed about on the desk, growling and squealing as the orgasm shot through her like a bolt of electricity. It shook her for almost half a minute, far longer than she had ever known such ecstasy. As the orgasm subsided, she shrieked again, but this time out of real pain. Frantically wriggling free of the thing, which now seemed to be ripping her apart, she collapsed on the desk with a sob, dripping with sweat and juices. Nessim kneeled to comfort her. From time to time she writhed involuntarily in the afterglow of intercourse, no longer from agony but from enormous satisfaction. It was the aftermath of an excitement maintained at a pitch that was only just physically bearable. There was pain in it, but it was a delicious pain that she could endure. It would pass.

And so it did, as Nessim covered her naked back with admiring kisses. Then it was just perfect. Then it was total euphoria.

CHAPTER FIVE

"Monsieur Legrand? Could I have a word with you?" Katharine was back at the office again, looking prim in a white blouse and flowered skirt. She'd timed her descent on the boss's office to coincide with the coffee break of his dour secretary. The woman took one every morning at eleven and returned ten minutes later looking just as dour.

Mr. Legrand distractedly waved her into the office. He was a private man to whom she had rarely spoken. Whenever she did, he insisted it be in French, so she did her best now, utilizing a feminine charm that had not previously been in her arsenal. She needed to know what, if anything, the big boss knew.

"C'est Monsieur Lenoir. Nicolas. I've just been working on this upcoming auction for him, and I was..." – luxurious hair toss – "...*wondering* if you've heard from him. I haven't been able to reach him on the phone. Was he supposed to be in the office this week?" Appropriately innocent, she thought, appropriately Kama-Sutra-*huh?* Legrand terrified her – this situation terrified her – but it wasn't as if he was going to fire her for being charming. She had to know where she, and Nicolas, stood.

"Forget about Monsieur Lenoir," Legrand said coldly. She was almost as taken aback by this as by fact that he had spoken in precise English. "You've been here for quite a few months now. Surely you can handle whatever needs to be done without having your hand held by our illustrious *Monsieur Lenoir*."

Without another word he looked back down to the papers on his desk, and Katharine dismissed herself, deflated. Nicolas was still in trouble, and the longer she dallied, the worse the trouble would get. Her glorious weekend was over and the central problem had returned, although after her experience with Nessim, it was one she knew she could manage. Nessim had made her feel capable, and she would simply have to use the astonishing force that she had discovered inside to fix the problem.

During lunch she executed phase one of her new plan. Arnaud had an extra set of keys to Nicolas' office, she knew. He had been at the auction house for several years, and although he hadn't wangled a promotion (despite his slimiest efforts), he was still the senior research assistant and had all of the responsibilities which that noble title conferred. Of course she didn't like thinking of the man, much less talking to him, but when he stayed behind during lunch, likely spying a chance for promotion in Nicolas' absence, she took the opportunity to swish over to him and girlishly hop up onto his desk. His look of eager astonishment alone was almost worth the performance.

"Like that tie, Arnaud," she cooed. "You've probably got some secret chic tailor whose name cannot be spoken, don't you?"

"Well, I…" he stammered. She saw the thoughts clearly on his face and could even translate them: first, *is she flirting with me?*; second, *my girlfriend bought the tie, but…*; third, *I'll hint at secret tailors*, and; fourth, *she totally wants me.* A ridiculous smile covered his face, and he smoothly continued with the confidence of his conclusions: "Funny you should mention it, but…."

"Actually I wanted to ask you about the auction," Katharine interrupted, letting her heel dangle from her foot, then snapping it back up so that he couldn't help but look. His eyes wormed all the way up to her intentionally bared thighs, which gave her ample opportunity to say all of this: "I've been working with Nicolas on some of the research, as I'm sure you know – *lesser* research, I guess – and anyway he's not here, and Monsieur Legrand couldn't give me any indication of when he *will* be here, so I was wondering if I could borrow your keys so I can recuperate that research."

"Keys?" the man said dumbly to her breasts.

"To Nicolas' office," she snapped.

"Of course," he murmured, reluctantly turning from the sight of her to rummage around in a sad drawer filled with sad things. He found the keys, whose location she duly noted, and dangled them in front of her with a grin that she assumed was meant to be devastating. "Thanks, Arnaud!" she sung before snatching the keys from his hand and flouncing off out of sight. This hot sex thing was turning out to be an asset.

Once she was in the office, she shut the door and immediately got to work. First she pulled out a somewhat relevant file from the pile on the desk, in case she found herself needing cover. The other files were all business too, she saw quickly, and made no mention of books full of delicious secret sex codes. Which she had cracked, by the way. Thank you very much.

So to the drawers, which weren't much help either, because apparently Mister Lenoir kept the entire history of art, as well as his many dealings with it, neatly organized in his head. "Nicolas!" she sighed. "Where the hell are you?" Spinning slowly in his chair, she thought: *So what if I cracked the code. I still don't have the faintest idea what it means.* As she turned, her eye fell upon an envelope peeking out of the corner of a leather writing pad that covered much of the desk's surface. Bending up the leather, she slid out the envelope, which was all that was hidden beneath. It was a bill from EDF, the French electricity company, and it was in the name of Nicolas Lenoir. Also, it had an address.

Exhilarated, she scribbled down the address on a scrap of paper and danced out of the office, locking it behind her. Then she glided past Arnaud's desk and dropped the keys down onto it without uttering a word.

It was a long afternoon. She was desperate to escape and find the place where she hoped she would find Nicolas, but she didn't dare risk calling any further attention to herself, particularly after her awkward conference with Monsieur Legrand. So she tried to appear normal, not that "normal" meant much of anything anymore. She rebuffed the flirtations of the men in the office with that innocent confusion that was now a conscious performance. They were all over her that day, it seemed, and she wondered whether she was unwittingly putting out different vibes. She took refuge in the library, where she would be left alone, and where she could research the Kama Sutra unobserved. She didn't know what she hoped to find, because there was honestly nothing to discover but sixty-four positions, and Richard Burton's translation, and other academic trivia, but she felt diligent doing the research and it passed the time.

The address was near the Pantheon in the Fifth Arrondissement, and although she remembered Nicolas mentioning that he lived in the Seventh, her curiosity was so acute that she practically raced through the streets once she had been released from work. The apartment was on one of the side streets that wound down from the Pantheon towards the

Place Contrescarpe – first floor, the envelope had said, which she knew meant second floor to American. That simple knowledge made her happy to be in Paris again, overjoyed to be at home in the City of Lights, and content with all that she had learned about herself in her short time there. The night was warm, the cafes were full. She was in love with it all, and she knew that it was in love with her too. Had to be.

Once she found the address, however, she was just plain nervous. How many strange buildings had she stood before over the past several days? Those experiences had been surprising, to say the least, but she wasn't sure that she was ready for another surprise, so she stood there on the opposite side of the street looking up at a lighted window. And she stood, and she stood. What had she been expecting? For Nicolas to run out, throw his arms around her, and thank her profusely for all the great detective work. Well that obviously wasn't going to happen.

She crossed the street to investigate further, an old hand now at the buzzer name game. None of them were Lenoirs, and the place for the name on the first floor had been left blank. She didn't dare press the button. This was risky, coming here based on a hidden envelope. She had doubted Nicolas' strategy ever since he had stopped picking up his phone, but maybe he was working his own angles, and she didn't want to interfere with that. So she crossed the street again and waited. And waited, her eyes fixed on the lighted window made brighter now by the lengthening shadows.

Finally she was rewarded for her patience. Someone materialized in the window. A silhouette appeared, and her excitement was such that she almost called up to it in joy. Quickly, however, she saw that the form was most definitely not Nicolas. It was a woman, a beautiful one from what she could see. She was talking on a telephone, looking out at the late afternoon. Katharine couldn't see her clearly, but she appeared to be dressed in a suit. Her skin was pale, and her hair was long, dark, and curled. That was about it. Then the phone dropped away and the woman disappeared. Katharine kept watch for another quarter hour, but nothing else happened. He wasn't there. She felt it. And she could not risk introducing herself to a woman she didn't know, she thought glumly. She had promised to keep their secret. She felt like a secret lover, except she wasn't.

And maybe Nicolas had nothing to do with the apartment in the first place. Maybe he had kept the envelope in order to return it to the electricity company, because it had been sent by mistake. But then how had he gotten the envelope in the first place if he didn't have access to the apartment? Answer me that, Miss Bright. So she wasn't crazy, but there was a beautiful woman in the apartment instead of Nicolas Lenoir. Was that a victory of detection? If so, it felt hollow, so she gave up on detection for the day to walk towards home and a stiff drink

The light was beginning to fade in the sky when she reached the Jardins du Luxembourg and decided to take a quick stroll through the park to see some greenery and clear her head. She loved the Jardins and would often spend long weekend days there, lounging in the sun or reading a book. She loved it because it often appeared in the books she read, as famous as it was, and it made her feel as if she was participating in a glamorous novel of her own. She decided that instead of waiting for home for that drink, she would have a glass of wine at the café near the entrance before it closed. So she took a seat on one of the green metal chairs, ordered, and stared out at the deepening shadows beneath the trees.

On a bench next to her, a scruffy young hippy was playing a guitar. She didn't notice him at first, but then the song captured her ear. It was a slow, sad tune, and he played it with raw feeling. It reminded her of lonely nights and broken hearts, and although she had a million things to dutifully worry about, she found herself completely overcome by the music, and now it was about her lonely nights and her broken heart. Silly, really, but she was just overcome. She watched the guitar player, sunk down in his sad dream, and as the sound drifted through the air, straight into her heart, she discovered that there was a tear rolling down her face.

It wasn't sadness, really. It was just a surfeit of emotion, a wonderful fullness that needed to spill out. And so she was weeping, grinning at those silly tears, but weeping. She let the song play through her, tears dripping uncontrollably from her chin. These last days…. She didn't know what to make of them. There was still much of her that was terrified by what she had been through, but she was also just so *grateful*. She had discovered so much, and there was still so much to discover. And it wasn't just about sex – not at all. It was about life and finding the secret of making it unpredictable and glorious again. This was a search worth dedicating herself to, she was convinced, and she wept even harder - with sadness, with joy - as if crying the last of the old Katharine out of her to emerge bathed and new. And when the song had ended, that was exactly how she felt. She dabbed at her cheeks with the back of her hand, left her glass of wine untouched, and walked out of the park.

In the streets she felt as if she had acquired a million new nerve endings. Every passing car or bike sent a shudder through her. She felt raw and free and open to the coming night. She felt it deep in her loins, and she felt the creeping excitement of a new lust. She stared into the faces of the people she passed and looked for her lust reflected. Her body felt honed like a knife, and she walked a few blocks before realizing that she had walked them following an attractive man. Laughing to herself, she turned down another street, but there were men there too, legions of men passing by to make her shudder. She let herself imagine. She imagined being in control, and cornering them, and taking them by force at her will. She wanted to create rather than be created. She wanted to be in control.

Another block, and she was thinking about what Nicolas had once told her: that she needed to learn how to really "see". He could judge a painting in a glance, but she had always needed to rely on the research, burying her head in histories and not seeing anything at all. So she practiced "seeing", staring deeply into the faces of passersby, even when their eyes met hers. In some way this was even more exciting than those nights of walking with the knowledge that she wasn't wearing a bra or underwear, and the more intently she looked, the more she found there was to see. In her romantic life she had always found herself with obviously attractive men, and so there had been a whole vast category of "unattractive" ones who had even scared her a bit, if only because they weren't ordinarily attractive. Now, however, the closer she looked, the more she discovered that there might be many other angles of desire. In fact, although not every man she passed could spark her imagination, she found that if she dropped the reins of her mind and just looked intently, most of them did.

There was one with a scar on his chin who looked harried and poor, but there was a manic energy in his step that got her feeling manic too. A teenager with a mop of hair and a slouch who might well shock her with his beauty if he stood up straight. And he would, if she commanded it. She had no doubt about that. A black African, tall and proud, with eyes that were beautiful but lost. They wouldn't stay lost for long if she gave him something to find. Beauty was being redefined for her as she walked. Beauty was changing because she was *looking*, and looking made her want to feel it too. It made her want to feel it tight against her and taste it with her mouth.

So pick one and hunt him down, this new voice said inside. She did not question the voice. She bared her teeth and began to follow a businessman walking south towards Montparnasse. How did one rape a man? She would find out and relish the experience. He had a cute ass, by the way, and that was just plain old ordinarily attractive. And although she couldn't see much of the rest of him, he walked with a confidence you could almost call a strut. She would see about the rest of him when they got there. Where was there? She had no idea, but she had a vision of following him into a dark alley and pressing him up against a wall to drink deep kisses and find the more delicious parts of him with her hands. That thought made her instantly wet.

Picking up the pace to narrow the gap between them, she thought in wonder: *I'm actually going to do this thing*. It was fun to be a predator. It was fun to know that you were a sexual guarantee. She wondered why she wasn't more afraid, but in her raw, excited state, she didn't wonder for long. The man turned into a narrower street, and she followed without hesitation, like a panther on the prowl. She could almost reach out and touch him now, and she ached to feel lips on hers and his hand between her thighs. She ached to corner him in a hot embrace and take his cock in her hand. She would suck him as she had sucked Nessim, she thought to herself, and paused for a moment to silence her jangling emotions. The streetlamps died out at the end of the street, and the man began to enter the darkness. She set off after him again, her heels confidently striking the cobblestones. This was it. This was now.

She was in the darkness now, moving towards him in a silence broken only by their approaching steps. Her cunt was an inferno that could not be extinguished, and her nipples tingled beneath her blouse.

And then her phone rang, and the hunt was shattered. She couldn't silence the ringing fast enough. The man turned to glance momentarily at her form in the darkness, and then he walked on towards the same old places and the same old things. Frustration overwhelmed her, and she nearly broke into tears again, but she had to pick up that phone. If there was any chance it was Nicolas, she had to pick up the phone.

It was Harriet. Just Harriet. She had news of Anita, she said, and she needed to see Katharine immediately.

The man was gone, and yes, she would have to see Harriet. She turned back up the narrow street, back into the rush hour swell, and headed towards the Seine. It wasn't far to the gallery.

"Lock the door behind you if you would," she heard Harriet call out as she entered the deserted space. The lights were still on, but it was closing time, and Harriet appeared at the railing of the loft above. "I'm up here."

Katharine turned the lock on the door and slowly moved across the gallery, idly taking in the photographs as if there might be clues to find in each of them. Then the portrait of Anita in the corner. She paused for a moment to look at it, thinking of Nicolas standing there next to the woman not more than a week earlier. Anita – she was still as beautiful as she had been the first time. Her glory hadn't faded one bit. And Katharine reluctantly admitted that John Salt could take one hell of a photograph. The thought of the randy photographer brought on a momentary panic, and she stupidly looked around the room for nude photos of herself. There weren't any, but it frightened her that she hadn't considered the possibility. Then she climbed the metal staircase to hear what strange Harriet would have to say.

Harriet was standing at a large table filled with photographs, pacing back and forth on a white shag carpet in her bare feet. She had obviously been happily working there for a while, and took a moment before turning to greet Katharine with a radiant smile. The smile was so spontaneous that it took Katharine aback, and she found herself returning the smile just as spontaneously. She had thought the woman was only hard edges and cold beauty, but in that moment Harriet looked as if she might actually be capable of fun. She really was beautiful. Yes, it was a somehow forbidding beauty, like one of those exotic flowers that were carnivorous and could devour an animal whole, but Katharine had loved art long enough to appreciate the woman's originality. She wore a simple black sack dress cut extremely high on her thighs, but the shapeless material only served as a contrast to what you knew was a finely honed body beneath. And those legs? Long, thin but sharply toned, and tan as copper. You looked at those legs for a moment and decided that she was probably tan like that all over. Katharine was surprisingly glad that she had come.

Harriet seemed to read her mind. "You look surprised," she said, as she stepped neatly over from the table to kiss Katharine on both cheeks.

"I guess I'm just curious to hear what you've discovered," Katharine said, and Harriet took her by the hand to lead her over to the table.

"Salt's assistant brought these over," she said, nodding down towards the table.

"Selena," Katharine murmured, nodding furiously. Salt had lied again, of course.

There were a dozen photos of Anita laid out, and they gave you a better sense of the woman. If possible, she was even more bewitching than Katharine had already known her to be. In each of the photos she was nude, and in several she looked as if she had just had sex, or was about to. Some were outright dirty – as dirty as Salt's photographs of Katharine had been – but in each she looked radiant and preternaturally confident, as if sex was just one of the myriad ways she might play with you. If a secret cache of nude photos of Ava Gardner in her heyday was one day found, Katharine thought, they would look exactly like this.

"Selena, yes," Harriet eventually said, looking down at the photos too, with love. "I didn't know you knew her."

"What else do you know about Anita?" Katharine asked. "I have to find her, Harriet."

"I know that she is very beautiful," Harriet chuckled. "Look at those *hips*," she sighed, reaching across Katharine, brushing Katharine's arm to point out Anita bent over a sudsy bathtub, her head turned to laugh back at the camera as if the joke was on them. "I think she may be the most beautiful woman I've ever met," Harriet said, drawing back her hand to grab Katharine's elbow, as if she was made dizzy by the model's beauty.

"Met?" Katharine asked, turning to face Harriet, who was closer than expected.

"Met and more," Harriet purred, moving her hand up to stroke Katharine's arm, to fondle her shoulder. "She's rather famous, in some Parisian circles at least. She's known for taking off her clothes and making the most of things. I understand why you must be desperate to meet her. I was desperate for years." And then Harriet leaned forward and lightly kissed Katharine on the lips. Katharine drew back almost immediately, not offended by the woman's attentions – the kiss had been odd, although spontaneous enough – but still eager to learn more about Anita.

"Do you know where she lives?" Katharine asked breathlessly. "Do you know where she hangs out? Do you know who she sees? I just need to talk to her. That's all. It's not even for me, really. It's for a friend of mine, and I know she can help him."

"I don't know anything more," Harriet said, turning back to study the photos and draping an arm around Katharine's narrow waist. "Not much, anyway. Although that might not be the right way to put it."

Katharine stared dumbly down at the photos too, disappointed but marveling at the woman's body all the same. Hypnotized? Maybe, because she did not find it unusual in the slightest when Harriet said this: "Look at those breasts. Pure pleasure, my angel. Have you ever tasted a woman? Do you know what a pleasure that is?"

Katharine turned to look without fear at the striking gallerist. This woman had a knowledge from which Katharine could learn. She had secrets she was still keeping, and if she had known Anita's body, Katharine was convinced that she knew much more. She stared deeply into the woman's dark and delighted eyes. After her hunt through the streets of the Fifth Arrondissment, it was as if she could not feel fear anymore. Sex was something that happened to people. People were something that happened to people. Harriet leaned forward and kissed her passionately on the mouth.

Katharine did not recoil. It couldn't be said that she returned the kiss, exactly, but she observed it with fascination. Harriet's hand was at her neck, teasing down the skin of her chest towards her breasts as they kissed again, and Katharine merely observed, as if this was a photograph, as if none of it was happening to her. Then Harriet's sharp hip found a space between Katharine's legs, and Katharine kissed back. She was bewildered with herself, but then that was nothing new, so she forced herself to stop thinking and *feel*, and then god it felt good.

Harriet moved so slowly that it all seemed like a dream, but soon enough her hand had slid down Katharine's shirt to fondle a breast, and Katharine kissed back harder, at Harriet's lips and at her neck. Then in slow motion Harriet stepped away to remove her dress. It came off so easily, so naturally, and yes, she was tan all over. If she was forty, she didn't look it. She was hard and limber and surprisingly beautiful. Her breasts were small but firm, her nipples pert and dark, the size of quarters. Her black g-string was off in a flash, and yes, yes, she was tan all over, as if she had been dipped in smooth milk chocolate. Girlishly she turned for Katharine to see her ass, muscled and high beneath that long sweep of sharp back, and then she turned again, and Katharine could not take her eyes from the woman's pussy, which was shaved bare and as tan as the rest of her.

"You think I'd make a good photograph?" Harriet asked, but Katharine didn't answer. She had stepped forward, propelled by some uncontrollable instinct, and had wrapped her arms around the woman's hard body for another deep kiss. Thirstily, her tongue flicked into the woman's mouth, and her shirt was off before she realized it. This only became clear when Harriet wrenched her mouth away from the kissing to lick a bared nipple. Katharine looked down in wonder at the sight of this strange and naked woman pleasuring her so expertly and fumbled for the zipper of her skirt. The skirt caught at her heels, and they both tumbled to the shag carpet, giggling into each other's mouths. Katharine kicked the skirt away and happily submitted to the sensation of Harriet covering her face with kisses. She arched her back for Harriet to pull her shirt away and undo her bra with a practiced flick. Then the woman's wonderful body was pressing against the length of her flesh, and her hand was raking down her hip, down past elastic to embed itself in Katharine's underwear. She didn't need to hear Harriet's conquering cry to know that she was already sopping wet. Immediately there were fingers inside of her, manipulating her towards mindlessness. Only one thought impatiently lingered in her mind: why doesn't she just take them *off!*

She did soon enough, after removing her fingers from Katharine's cunt to lick them theatrically. And then she kissed down her chest, across her belly, down to the elastic of the underwear, which she took in her hands as she kept going down, kissing the sparse hair there, kissing her thighs, her knees, the sharp line of her shins, her feet, her red-painted toes. And then Katharine was laid out on the floor completely naked before the crouching Harriet, eyes closed and writhing for more.

Harriet wasn't so impatient. She paused for a moment to watch the girl, marveling at her beauty until she couldn't take it anymore and kissed back up those fabulous legs to that deliciously drenched cunt. She crawled like a cat, looking and kissing, until the cunt drew her like a magnet and she slid to the floor to lick and only lick.

She was a connoisseur and licked carefully at first, observing

Katharine's reactions. First she lowered her tongue, and with its point she traced the line where Katharine's thighs met the mound named after a goddess – Venus. She took her time, drawing back again to look, and to spread Katharine's knees all the way out with her hands, like a master chef preparing a flat surface to work upon. Katharine watched with fascination, her head hitched up off the carpet. Then Harriet's tongue moved in again to trace another line, probing into the more central ridge where the mound folded into her again. The flesh was softer, and slicker, here, and Katharine still held up her head to watch, clinically fascinated by the situation even as rampant desire began to tug at the edges of that fascination. Harriet licked up the right side, expertly flicked across the hood of her clitoris – merely making a brief formal introduction – and then back down the left side, all the way down, until she pressed into the taut skin between Katharine pussy and her anus. Perineum – that was the word. Katharine had read about its pleasures in women's magazines, but they had made it sound medical, whereas this was pure bliss. Harriet teased it with little flicks of the point of her tongue, and then she licked like a cat, letting Katharine feel the whole width of her tongue sliding over her most secret spot. Occasionally she would look up to meet the young American's eyes, and Katharine would gasp at the sight of the woman's beautiful intensity, as if she'd been struck by an arrow.

And Harriet was discovering more, peeling back the layers

of Katharine: her squiggled line of lips, which were already brushed with her own wetness. Gently, not yet wanting to break the final seal, teasing her as only a woman could, Harriet followed the line of those lips with her tongue, parting them just slightly and pausing every few seconds to wetly kiss parts she had already covered, all the way out to the smooth sweep of her thigh. Katharine was moaning with pleasure now. She had sped around the curve and was shocked to see an eighteen-wheeler orgasm bearing down upon her. Never had she moved through the stages of pleasure so quickly, at least not with another human being, and she hadn't even been penetrated and her clitoris had hardly been touched. She put a hand to Harriet's head to give herself more time. Harriet got the signal and moved her kisses up to Katharine's belly, slowly sliding the length of her own body up Katharine's, skin meeting skin everywhere it could, until their mouths met and Katharine was drinking her own taste from Harriet's mouth. She hesitated at first, holding back her tongue, but then the taste and the feel of this lithe woman gyrating over her was too intoxicating to be resisted. She wrapped her arms around Harriet and kissed deeply, letting her hands rove all over the impossibly hard body of this snake goddess of a woman. Then the snake goddess broke off of the salty kiss to wriggle back down to her main objective. Katharine felt the tongue lightly tap her anus, and she groaned with a mixture of fear and pleasure.

From her anus the tongue moved back up again, splitting

her middle ever so slightly until Harriet arrived again at her clitoris, sliding her tongue up into the hood, pressing the protective skin aside, circling it, slipping over it again, hard, as if she was trying to pin it down with a tack. Katharine began to gurgle with blind pleasure and let her head drop to the floor with a thunk. She tried to shake herself free of the maddening pleasure that had again come too quick, but Harriet held her in place, locking her hands around Katharine's waist, smothering her clitoris with every part of her tongue. Harriet kissed it ardently, as if it was a lover she hadn't seen in months, finally tonguing past the lips, deep into an endless sea of wet. Katharine's body bucked uncontrollably up against Harriet's chin as the lesbian fucked her expertly with her tongue, deeper and deeper, as if she would not be content until that tongue was permanently lodged in Katharine's heart.

She slid back over the elastic wall inside, then out to stab at Katharine's clitoris, then back deep inside, her teeth occasionally pressing into the soft ridges of flesh. Katharine thrashed with pleasure. Harriet controlled her body, and then it was just shuddering, shuddering, shuddering, locked in an endless, shattering orgasm.

After resting a moment, they kissed for a while, their breasts meshed, their legs intertwined. It seemed to Katharine that she hadn't felt such peace in years. Harriet was completely feminine now, smiling adoringly, and Katharine couldn't resist kissing her and kissing her. Harriet returned the kisses passionately, as Katharine's hands moved to feel her breasts – so firm, so delectable. She nestled down past Harriet's neck to kiss the nipples, which were as hard as pearls. She licked them, taking enormous pleasure in discovering what made the wind rush out of Harriet's mouth. Then Harriet was pushing her head further down and hissing: "Kiss it kiss it Katharine."

On her knees now, looking down at Harriet's perfectly shaven slit, Katharine spread the woman's legs as had been done to her. She hesitated for a moment, looking up towards Harriet's face again, but the woman's eyes were closed and her head was already lolling about in anticipation of Katharine's tongue. The sight of this spurred Katharine on, and she tentatively dropped her mouth to the shining opening. Once again it was something that she had never done before but knew exactly how to do. She was an innocent but an expert, schooled herself by a dozen men's tongues. And so she began to lick, expecting a taste that was distinctly *woman*, but there was no taste there, just an enticing moisture that seemed to lap greedily back at Katharine's licking lips. The hairlessness of Harriet fascinated her, and she let her lips glide all over the swelling vulva, which was as smooth as Harriet's perfect cheek. Her doubts removed, Katharine began to lick with purpose as her own pussy wetted in harmony with the one she now attacked with a selfish passion. The excitement of making a woman squirm beneath her face was powerful, and she wanted more. She wanted tits and pussies everywhere, and she wanted to make them squirm.

Harriet bucked up into her mouth with the force of a mad-woman, but her strength was no match for Katharine's, whose long, strong muscles held the woman in place with a sort of sadistic satisfaction. Harriet snarled and cried like a trapped animal, her tongue darting out between bared teeth to lick at something imaginary in the air. Then her dams were over-whelmed by the rush of love spurting through her, and Kath-arine reared back to watch the waterfall, still thirsty for more, her palm posed on Harriet's firm belly as the woman went insane, then found herself again, slowly, before reaching up to bring Katharine's face to hers another time.

They kissed like this for a while and gently traced each other's bodies with their fingers. Katharine thought idly about cat-egories – straight, lesbian, bi, whatever – and thought of how foolish all that was when two bodies were lying naked to-gether. Was she bi, then? Who cared? She had spent enough of her life seeking the safety of categories, and she refused to let categories define her anymore.

What she did know was that she liked Harriet after all, and she liked licking her pussy, and she liked looking at her strange feminine beauty. Harriet could be trusted, she thought to herself, and before she had even realized it, she was speaking the words in her head aloud. Her head on Harriet's breast, her body extended across the soft carpet, she began telling everything. She talked about Nicolas and the trouble that she was trying to help him with – that was why she had come into the gallery looking for Anita the week before. She left out the part about the stolen Kama Sutra, but said that Nicolas had been unjustly accused of a crime, and how horrible that had been. Then there was John Salt. What an uncomfortable experience. Did he act so entitled with every woman?

"Not me," Harriet smiled, and then Katharine was smiling too, telling her about a clue she'd found that might make everything right if she could just find this Anita. Yes, she sighed, somehow she had to find Anita. With this they fell into silence again. Harriet looked at her inquisitively, as if she had expected the story to continue. When it didn't, she abruptly raised herself to her elbows, still grinning – lasciviously.

"But you left out Nessim Hosnani entirely! I was looking so forward to hearing about *that*. That man is rarely impressed, but he assured me that if I could just get your skirt off, then you would prove *delectable*. Well he was right, wasn't he?"

Katharine couldn't believe her ears. She snapped up off the floor, eyes shooting daggers at Harriet. Rage overtook her, all the libidinous rage of her manhunt, wild emotions coalescing into a blinding rage, and she drew back her hand and slapped the woman's face as hard as she possibly could.

Instead of retaliating, Harriet sat there calmly, flushing with what almost looked like pleasure. The sight disgusted Katharine. "What is going on?" she cried. "You knew *everything*! You *used* me! So what is it? What do you want with Nicolas and me?"

"I. Can't. Tell you," Harriet said defiantly, sticking out her angular chin as if daring Katharine to slap it again. The sight of this enraged Katharine further, and swinging her arm all the way back (as the lanky girl on the tennis courts of Portsmouth had once done), she slapped Harriet again, this time with astonishing force. Instead of ducking, Harriet braced herself for it, the cords of her neck standing out as she took the full impact of the blow. Her chin hardly moved as her cheek was stained a violent red. Katharine watched in horror as that lascivious grin quickly spread across Harriet's face, and she hissed: "Again."

Katharine ran. She grabbed her clothes, snatched up a handful of Anita's photos, and she ran.

"If you find Anita, tell her I asked about her," she heard Harriet cry as she dressed herself and fumbled with the lock. Then she was running again.

CHAPTER SIX

She could work. She could work so hard that she forgot about everything else, arriving early and intending to stay late. She could lose herself in figures and facts, but eventually the panic would return. She was being watched, they were playing with her, and she was no closer to knowing who "they" were than she had been on the night of Bastille Day, when Nicolas had called asking her to investigate. Where the hell was he? Why didn't he pick up the phone? And why was it that the only direction one could ever go was forward, and that forward meant putting herself out there again? *Stop with these stupid questions*, she thought to herself, and as soon as she had a chance she slipped out of the office.

At home she paced the rooms, too agitated to dance. Fucking Nessim! How could he have told Harriet about their afternoon? How could he have *gossiped?* He had been so...*nice*, but now she was just furious with him. With every step her fury blazed higher, and she cursed Nessim, cursed his smile, cursed his dildos, cursed his cock, that cock, cursed the taste of it in her mouth, cursed her wetness, her body, her lust and the whole wide world. And when she had finished, she cursed herself

again, because despite all her curses, the release of emotions
had achieved an unexpected effect, and her hand was at her
breasts again, at her neck, as she thought of that awful and
sexy Nessim. He wouldn't hurt her. Nessim would never hurt
her, and she absolutely had to see him again.

"Oh *me!*" she said aloud. Forward was the only way to go.
First, however, she could do with a nice warm bath, and so she
went into the bathroom and poured herself one. Warm baths
always restored her good mood, and although she cursed
herself some more for being so easily made happy again, she
figured she ought to take what she could get. Move forward,
take what you can get – yes, she had practically formulated
a life philosophy, and it wasn't even dinnertime. Grinning
at herself despite it all, she soaped herself from head to toe
and luxuriated in the feeling. She took her time and shaved
her legs. They hardly needed it, but she liked to feel smoothy
smooth. And then…her pussy? She had never done that before, but the thought of it excited her tremendously. Holding
her pelvis out of the water, she lathered some soap into the
hair there to test how serious she was. Mmm. That felt good
too. But a razor? Maybe if she was careful, she thought, and
tentatively touched the razor to the edge of her pubic hair.
Gently, she stroked upwards until bare skin appeared. She
stroked again and again, her pussy tingling with excitement.
She loved the look of it, she loved the feel of it, and so she
moved on inwards towards her labia, which she delicately

touched with the razor, fearing a cut (but fear only adding to the excitement). Methodically she shaved and shaved until the entire cunt was bare and pristine, and she looked down on it in admiration. She let her hand slide over its smoothness, which was as perfect as a breast, or an ass, or a cheek. She thought of Harriet's smooth pussy – delicious, infuriating Harriet – and she stroked and prodded until the stroking picked up rhythm and she was riding towards an orgasm that came so fast it left her breathless.

Michel came in from work as she was dancing out of the bathroom. "We've got dinner with some of the lawyers," he said as he set his briefcase down, paying her nudity no attention. She didn't like his professional tone, and she couldn't believe that he wasn't noticing her - again. All of her anger and frustration surged up again, and she fixed him with this fury, snarling: "That's it? And I'm just supposed to hop along? *No*, Michel! I am not a fancy possession. I'm not one of those books you keep nicely dusted on your shelves!"

"Baby," he sighed, then with great precision, as if expressing a universal truth that she was too stubborn or stupid to see: "You know how important these dinners are."

"Not to me," she spat, knowing that she was overreacting, but the thought of a dinner with Michel right now, much less with his smug colleagues, filled her with dread.

"Baby, what's wrong?" he cooed as he mechanically put his arms around her, repeatedly stroking her back as if she were a temperamental appliance you just had to jiggle the right way to fix. This enraged her further, and she began to scream – cursing Michel and his work and his ridiculous self-regard. Michel, of course, made a clear distinction between his colleagues and himself and didn't like to hear himself compared to them, which in his mind was a comparison that could only be unflattering. When it came to his own ego he was easily wounded, and this inevitably made him furious. Although he rarely deigned to lose his temper, now he shouted right back, hotly criticizing Katharine's selfishness, her disrespectfulness, her American stupidity, and even her cooking. She refused to listen and ran off to the bedroom, where she locked the door and flopped onto the bed. Michel went on screaming, banging at the door like some great big macho. *What a fraud!*, she thought as she covered her ears. Pretending to be the cool, enlightened lawyer. She would stay locked up in there for days if she had to. She didn't want to see his face, and she sure as hell wasn't going to any dinner.

Eventually Michel gave up, and she felt the front door slam. She took her hands from her ears and rolled onto her back. That figured. The jerk hadn't even noticed her shaven pussy.

So what's a girl to do alone for another night in the big city? She took the photos of Anita from her purse and spread them on the bed to peruse for a while. Half-consciously, she found her body gesturing towards the poses in the photographs, and she imagined herself folded like origami into the sixty-four positions of her own Kama Sutra. Sixty-four partners, sixty-four positions – they would unearth it from some crypt a century from now and marvel at the woman who had possessed such sexy secrets. She amused herself with this scenario for a while, and then she knew that it was time to move forward, yes forward, to tackle the mystery again. She also knew that like it or not, she had to see John Salt.

After dressing she went out into the dusk and caught a taxi for Montmartre. She had the driver stop on the Boulevard de Clichy at the corner of Salt's street and stepped into a café for a quick shot of courage – more precisely, a quick Pernod, whose strong licorice kick she had come to appreciate in courage situations. Her first awkward weeks of Paris parties would have been significantly more excruciating without the stuff, and so she and the drink had a certain trust.

She stood at the bar, scanning the headlines as was her habit, glancing up occasionally to gaze out at the oncoming night. She was paying the bill when John Salt sauntered slowly past the windows. "Merci!" she said to the bartender, and as she skirted out the bar after Salt, she caught a glimpse of her reflection in the glass of the window. Her face was set in determination. She defied anyone to mess with Katharine Bright.

She followed him up the Boulevard de Clichy towards Pigalle, Paris's old red-light district, now upscaled for tourists but still attracting a fair amount of sludge. There were bright colored lights and half-naked girls beckoning from the deep, fluorescent entrances of theaters that were now strip clubs. Night had arrived, and adventurous tourists swiveled their heads in wonder. There were the desperate drunken-looking men too – the habitués. Without fail their strides slowed to watch Katharine swish by. She tried her best not to acknowledge them, eyes locked on John Salt, who strolled casually along as if touring the strip clubs was just his ordinary evening promenade. Occasionally he would stop to shake some guy's hand, which only confirmed Katharine's opinion of him. In the land of illicit sex, he was a local. Not that Katharine was a foreigner, she had to admit, but nevermind – tonight she was a detective.

"Check out the rack on her!"

Katharine made a mask of her face, wanting to make ants of the three American college boys who inventoried her body as they passed as if they were the only people in the world who might speak English. Why her? She was wearing a conservative black dress and in no way looked like an easy score, she thought to herself. It didn't occur to her that a week of Kama Sutra sex might send out its own vibrations. It didn't occur to her that she was the physical incarnation of the dreams that Pigalle was meant to manufacture.

When Salt turned to kiss a girl in spangles waving flyers, Katharine had to duck into the entrance of another club. There a stringy girl with sad eyes smiled at her uncertainly as Katharine made a show of studying a poster on the wall: "Sex Show. Brazilian girls. All night long." Thankfully Salt's stripper tour soon continued. She focused on him until her surroundings blurred and she was fully locked on the chase. She liked being a detective, she realized. For the second night in a row, she was tracking a man through the streets like a predator, and she liked it.

Then Salt turned down a shadowy side street, and she liked it somewhat less than she had the night before. But she followed, coming within a few dozen meters of him as he slowed then stopped to greet another girl who had appeared. He kissed her, they chatted, he shoved a ten euro bill into her flashy halter top and they both laughed. What kind of scruffy American artist threw that kind of money around on the street? This was an economic question she didn't have long to ponder, because Salt disappeared with the woman and Katharine moved after him to investigate.

The entrance was so nondescript that a casual passerby would never have picked it out. Next to a dim ticket booth there was a sign over a door: *Cleopatra's Dream*. Salt was nowhere to be seen, but the woman in the halter top was now behind the booth. A mustachioed man in a dingy suit and bad teeth stood beside her, and although the woman looked at Katharine suspiciously as she approached the booth, the man was only too happy to call out and offer her free entry tonight and every night forever. He slid a ticket through the slot, and Katharine took it. Feeling it in her hand, for the first time that night she wondered about her motivations. Yes, the detective act was amusing, and yes, there was still much to be learned from John Salt, but what exactly did she intend to learn? She asked the question directly to her body, since her body was the one that had been lately problematic. Her body didn't answer. It was coy about these things.

Bravely pushing through a door beside the booth, she was greeted by a solemn bouncer a head taller than she. She gave the man her ticket, and he took what seemed like five minutes to rip it in two, carefully looking her up and down. Then she was free, or trapped, in Cleopatra's Dream. She walked down a short corridor until she came to a thick red curtain, beyond which loud opera played. She didn't know her opera well, but it sounded like one of the arias from La Bohème, which Michel had taken her to see at the Bastille a month earlier, before taking her to dinner on the Place des Vosges and ruining the evening by singing his own little mock arias, ridiculing an experience that had moved her deeply. She found a slit in the curtain and split it to slip through.

She was in a small theater. On stage two women danced.

They were naked, their bodies impeccably toned, their dancing more like a set of gestures towards the opera rather than a fluid series of movements. Katharine stood there watching them as her eyes adjusted to the dark. They moved towards each other, intertwining arms and legs as a steady beat rose to back the aria, giving a rhythm to the dance that was overtly sexual. They kissed and they stroked as their legs scissored around each other.

Her eyes adjusting to the darkness now, Katharine looked around the theater. There were about a hundred and fifty seats and a dozen or so people scattered about, mostly men sitting alone, but a couple of accompanied women too. The room was too dim to pick out John Salt, so Katharine took a seat at the back to watch for him and observe the show, which was more professional than she ever could have imagined…and becoming increasingly erotic. The two women had pulled each other onto a thin mattress – yet another scenario Katharine had recently performed herself, she thought – and were now having a sort of stylized sex, kissing and fingering as they arched their hips into the air to give the audience the fullest glimpse of their firm asses and shaven pussies. Katharine found herself becoming aroused, partially because of the women's incredible erotic appeal, but also in the knowledge that her pussy was shaven too. Then another woman appeared from behind the curtain at the back of the stage and danced out towards the others to the pulsing beat. Her dance was carnal and savage – hips thrusting, hair sweeping the floor – and to another captivated blonde dancer sitting in the back of the theater, admirably executed. Katharine had never seen a woman dance with such sexual confidence. She would have been terrified to dance naked on stage herself, but this woman loomed over the other two like a ravenous Roman goddess, stepping high around them, sweeping in occasionally for a pinch or a suck. Her voluptuous body was astonishingly flexible, and Katharine found herself reminded of something, or somebody. Then a word leapt into her mind unbidden: "*Vif!*" And she knew that body, she knew that woman. Brigitte her dancing instructor apparently had a second job, and she was amazingly good at it.

Katharine's astonishment was quickly overtaken by another one as two magnificently oiled muscle men appeared from the wings and began to dance with Brigitte, lifting her into the air, bending her out into perfect splits. They locked hands to make a circle around her, and she frantically threw herself against them as if desperate to escape. Then she seemed to accept her fate and shimmied down into a crouch to begin tugging at the men's cocks, which she quickly made hard. This was not just a performance anymore, Katharine realized with a shiver. Colored lights roved over the dancers' bodies and they were fucking, really fucking. Katharine absently put a hand to her breast and stared dumbly, as if the pleasant, drunken buzz of the Pernod had just hit. Could they *do* this? Maybe in Paris.

Or maybe just down the backstreets in Cleopatra's Dream.

Soon she spied Salt in a seat halfway to the stage, nodding his head as if someone had just thrown a touchdown. Katharine sighed and stood to scurry down towards him, eyes still locked on the undulating Brigitte, holding on for a moment longer to that enticing vision. Salt, of course, was a buzz kill. He nodded without surprise as she slid down his row to slump – as inconspicuously as possible, fearing the eyes of Brigitte – low into the chair next to his. Had he been watching her from the moment she entered? Maybe she wasn't the detective she thought she was, and he had been leading her to the theater all along. She remembered the ten euros he'd slid into the camisole of the woman at the entrance and decided that this was a distinct possibility.

"Fancy meeting you here," she drawled as casually as she could, watching him out of the corner of her eye. He was so riveted by the onstage fucking that he took a long moment to respond. Then there was this, delivered with that boyish John Salt grin: "I'm a long-standing member. Not really, but if you want to meet a long-standing member...." He took her hand and put it to his crotch. Yep, her hand reported back: it was standing. Snatching it away, she hissed: "You lied to me! You shared photos of me! Without my permission!"

"Please refrain from talking during the performance," he said without looking at her. She sighed and said: "I need your help, John."

His eyes shining with amusement, he put an index finger to his lips and shushed her.

"I take it you come here often," she grumbled.

"I find some of my best models here," he whispered. "Look at that one, for example. I mean look at that ass."

"Yep," Katharine nodded. The ass was spectacular. She thought it best not to mention that the woman's name was Brigitte. Her instinct told her that a girl should never mention her friends to John Salt. "Aren't you even going to ask me what I'm doing in a place like this?"

"Baby, I gave up that pickup line in the third grade," he said distractedly, his attention occupied by the stage again. "Got me into a world of trouble with a pair of cute little fifth-grade twins, and I had the wisdom to retire it right then and there." She giggled despite herself. There was apparently a woman inside of her who found John Salt charming. Either that, or she herself – whoever that was – had just realized that John Salt was, in fact, charming. Still charming as he put his hand to her knee? Yep, even then. What the hell.

They sat that way for a minute or so, losing themselves in the performance that was not a performance. Brigitte had the men laid out on the stage beneath her now, and she danced above them on her toes as if she was wearing sharp and emasculating heels. Katharine thought of the time she had danced naked in front of her windows, and she went mushy just thinking of dancing like that again, over two oiled and muscled men with hard cocks in their hands. She glanced furtively over at John. His other hand was fondling his crotch. She stared down at his hand on her knee and stupidly felt like a high school girl again, wondering if he'd make a next move, and whether she wanted him to. Looking at him inquisitively, she realized that he was no longer watching the stage. He had turned to watch a middle-aged couple sitting on the far end of their row. They were kissing passionately as the man unbuttoned the woman's shirt and brought out an enormous pale breast to suckle. The woman's eyes were fixed on the stage as he did this, her hand fumbling blindly at his zipper. The man's cock appeared, a glint of flesh at his lap. Once the woman felt it in her hand, she turned from the stage and lowered her mouth to the cock, her eyes cast up to look directly at Salt as she sucked with abandon. Onstage was an orgy now, but Katharine was riveted by this couple, whose clandestine exhibitionism she found even more exciting. To take that risk…. And that woman! She wasn't beautiful but she was fabulous! Her dark eyes crossed Katharine's, and Katharine felt as if she'd just been kissed.

Then she realized that her own lap had been bared, and that

Salt's hand was gripping the inside of her thigh. She pushed his hand back down her knee and smoothed her skirt, thinking: *I have beautiful legs* – as if she hadn't realized it before. It was as if her own awakening body was the performance now, and she watched it in fascination. Salt was watching it too, ravenously, and so was the cocksucking woman a half dozen seats away, and so was the man. Salt resumed caressing the inside of her thigh, working her skirt up to her panties again. She pushed him away, watching herself. No, she couldn't expose herself here in that way. It was far too public, and she was terrified of being found out. By whom? Michel, who likely hadn't been to Pigalle since age seventeen? Brigitte, who was gloriously without shame? Salt, who had found her out days ago? The lusty couple down the row? She didn't know. Frustrated, she spread her legs slightly, just to see. She thought of that night at the café by Maubillon, when she had let a man look up her skirt. Salt's hand crept up again, and she watched it in fascination.

She felt terribly exposed, but it was dark in there, after all, and Salt's hand was like a fact she had to accept, and did. It was more insistent now, tracing the contours of her pussy through her underwear. She wanted to hide, or she wanted to be stripped onstage. Her mind reeled, and his hand stroked, and she felt as if this was what she had been made for, this moment: John Salt's hand edging her panties aside to touch her moistened pussy. *Yes*, she sighed, sliding lower in her chair to press harder against his hand. Her eyes closed against the world as her head fell back contentedly against the cushion. Salt had two fingers in her, three. His lips were at her neck. Her eyes snapped open. The woman – what was she up to now? Still sucking her companion's cock, taking it deep, but with her eyes gobbling up the sight of Salt and Katharine, who stared right back, mirroring the woman's lust. Katharine kept looking, and now she wanted the woman to see. Then onstage: Brigitte had her back to the audience and two cocks in her mouth. Katharine had never been so excited in her life. All the world was a stage, all its men and women were players, and all its players were fucking.

When Salt removed his hand from her pussy to loosen the belt of her dress, she replaced his fingers with hers to continue the stroking. The dress slipped off her shoulder, and a bra strap followed close behind, sliding down to her elbow until both breasts were bared. With her free hand she quickly covered them again with the loosened flaps of her dress before Salt intercepted the hand and placed it back at the beginning, at his crotch. Onstage Brigitte had a man inside her now and a pussy at her mouth. Spellbound, Katharine watched her lips working tightly over the thing, and undid Salt's zipper, then the button at his pants. He helped her hoist his hardened cock from the gap, and she began to stroke it without taking her eyes from Brigitte. Meanwhile Salt slipped his hand into her dress and began to massage her breasts, his eyes locked on the stage as well. From a few rows back they could have been an ordinary couple enjoying an ordinary evening at the theater.

But others had seen their manipulations, others beside the exhibitionist couple. Katharine was so riveted by the magnetic poles of Salt's cock and Brigitte's body that she did not realize it at first, but a man had come into the theater and had sat in their row. There was only a one-seat gap between her and him. She did not notice this: the man was older and graying, with the battered ears and nose of a former boxer. He wore a shabby suit and outdated tie and watched the stage intently. He was sensing Katharine Without looking, he was feeling her lust and her beauty beside him.

Salt was kissing her neck, rolling a nipple between his thumb and forefinger, when she felt another hand on her thigh. Blind with desire now, her body seething with sensations, it took her a moment to isolate the hand. Then, somewhere in the back of her mind, she realized that the hand was not Salt's, and she moved it away. Salt was kissing her mouth now. Her legs were spread further for the glorious feel of his hand beneath her skirt, and she was hypnotized by his cock, which was now slick, and over which her hand moved tightly, as regular as a metronome. The woman down the row had now completely exposed her breasts, and her man had his pants down to his knees. They were no longer concerned by the eyes of others. Katharine felt the hand at her thigh again, and she moved it away. Salt moved the top of her dress slightly aside and began to lick her breasts. She sighed deeply, a sound that was drowned out by the music. The hand had appeared at her thigh again, and although it horrified her, she let it stroke her. It was a soft and reverent hand. She could not stop it, even as the man moved into the seat next to hers. Ten fingers at her pussy, Salt's and the man's, and she simply could not stop it. She could walk away, but she did not want that. She wanted this, and she knew in her bones that the only escape was on the other side of pleasure.

Brigitte was sucking the other man's cock now onstage, and Katharine leaned over to lower her mouth to Salt's. He held her head there and groaned, giving no indication at all that she was still a beginner at the practice. He tasted different from Nessim – randier and more pungent – but the beery taste was not unpleasant. It excited her even, just the taste alone, simply because it was associated with such an outrageously exciting act. Down the row the other woman's eyes locked eyes with hers as she returned to licking the man's member. They were crazy eyes, the eyes of a mad seer, and Katharine let herself get lost in them for a moment until it was as if she was sucking both cocks herself, making both men writhe as they grabbed her hair.

As she had twisted in her seat to bring her mouth into Salt's lap, her pelvis had risen slightly up from the cushion so that her ass, with her dress bunched over it, now faced the stranger beside her, at whom she still refused to look. The position had drawn Salt's hand away from her pussy, sliding her panties back into place, but soon she felt the backs of her thighs being fondled again from behind. A hand dove beneath her skirt to insert itself between them, and it began to wriggle up towards her sopping cunt. Again she submitted to the touch, spreading her legs slightly to free the hand. It quickly edged her panties aside, and a thumb began to move in and out of her, pausing occasionally to pinch at her clitoris. She groaned and attempted to silence herself by taking in all of Salt's dick, pressing it back towards the wall of her throat until she gagged and thrust her head from it, gasped, and recommenced the licking. The thumb in her pussy was sending waves of hot need through her now. She reached back towards the man, and found another hand that guided hers down towards his lap, and a naked cock that protruded from the rough material of his pants. She felt the cock – far smaller than Salt's, uncircumcised and half-limp. She began to stroke it, drawn in two directions by the fascination of two live penises, which was a sensation she had never known. She didn't care who saw her now.

She had no idea what mad configuration was now being demonstrated onstage, but the beat had fallen from the music again, and it was just a piercing aria rising in pitch. She raised her head from Salt's pulsing, saliva-slicked dick and eased back into her chair. She turned her eyes to the stage again, reaching out to recapture Salt's lap, so that she now had a cock in each hand. It was as if she was at the controls of an orgiastic spaceship. She was the captain, she thought with a salacious grin, and she could take them anywhere. On-stage Brigitte was in control too, sitting on her knees with her hands reaching up to fondle the men on either side of her. She looked out at the audience, and for a moment Katharine was certain that they had recognized one another, but they were mirror images now, and it didn't matter. The men on either side of Katharine groaned in unison. They weren't seeing anything at all. She looked down across her exposed breasts to the leaping daggers of flesh, and she grinned, stroking even faster. The opera singer soared up to her highest notes, and Brigitte's men were responding to her touch by coming in great, violent spurts, spattering Brigitte's body with hot, relieved drops. And Katharine was a mirror image, and her cocks were coming too. She hooded each with her hands and felt the hot stream of juices against her palms. Then they were done, and she cleaned her hands on their cocks, their balls, and on the insides of their thighs. Then she was done, and she primly rebuttoned her dress and rose to sashay out of Cleopatra's Dream without glancing at anyone.

Back outside the world hardly seemed real. The colors seemed faded, and even the sound of the traffic was strangely muted. She paced up and down the street for several minutes, keeping an eye on the theater's entrance. She didn't want to run into Brigitte, the faceless man, or anyone else who might have gotten ideas about her, but she did need to see Salt. That's why she had come, after all, back when she had been a detective. He emerged soon encugh, and she laughed to see how discombobulated he was. He stood on the sidewalk shaking his head as if he had just been set back down on earth after an alien abduction. *They had the most erotic alien seductresses up there on Planet XXX....* She laughed again, gratified at having astonished the unflappable Salt.

"Fancy meeting you here," she called out from where she stood. She saw him grin, then turn to walk towards her.

"That's a damned good line," he drawled, recovering himself and making a comical show of formally shaking her hand. "I will admit that I underrated it. Yes, that is one highly effective pickup line."

"I'll keep that in mind," she cooed, flirty now despite the sordid orgy they had just concluded. She was pleased with herself and getting a kick out of her newfound charm. That, and her newfound double-cock-stroking technique.

"Can I walk with you for a while?" he asked almost innocently, to which she demurely nodded. They set off south towards the Grands Boulevards, walking in silence as they acclimated themselves to the old world. Eventually her mind began to circle back in on the questions that had been preoccupying her, and she asked him how he had gotten the book. And how was it possible that the book had not only been in his possession but that he had known she was looking for it? How in the world was that possible? Questions crowded her mind, and she found herself furious again.

"I didn't steal it," Salt said calmly. "I was more of a...middleman."

"Then who stole it?!" she cried, drawing the stares of pedestrians. "Nicolas, he's my boss, he's in real danger if I don't figure this out, John. Can't you understand that? Or are you the one behind it for some reason? That's what I can't figure out."

"Sounds like there's a lot more than that you can't figure out," he said, putting out an arm to keep her from walking out into a whizzing intersection.

She took a deep breath and tried to sound rational. She tried to sound like Katharine: "Well *somebody* stole it from the vault, John, and the house knows it's missing, so now I can't take it back. What about that? What do I do now about that book, *Mister Middleman?*"

"I wouldn't worry," he said lightly. "If there's one man who knows how to take care of himself, it's Nicolas Lenoir."

She shook her head as if she couldn't believe her ears. "You had the book, and you know Nicolas. Harriet too, of course, that lesbian…."

"*Lovely* woman, Harriet. Incidentally, very good at what she does."

"And probably Hosnani too for all I know, and…," well, she hadn't actually gotten the name of that detective.

"Nessim? Just socially. Cocktail parties and whatnot."

"John Salt: please just shut up for a minute. Fuck you. Are you hearing me? Fuck you and your mystery."

"Shocking language."

"And those photographs you took of me? Hell, keep them, if that's the sick kind of thing that turns you on. You can't blackmail me, if that's what you're after. I don't have any money, if that's what you want. And whatever else you might want, I more or less gave to you back in that theater, so please just make this stop."

Gripping her elbow in his powerful hand, he looked intently at her until she stopped raving. Eventually she focused, and she realized that they had already made it to the Pont Royal, where the Seine rushed darkly beneath their feet. She looked back up at Salt's face, and he said: "Katharine, I will not do anything that might hurt you, and you have to trust me when I say that you are on the right path. I can't say more – it's too risky for me – but you are on the right path. It's a big world. You and I have both moved over the face of it, and we are figuring out its mysteries. You've got to keep pushing on." Then he gently touched his lips to hers.

"So what do I do with the book?" she asked softly.

"The book?" he shouted out to the river, propelling her across the bridge with his hand. "Jesus, you *read* it, Katharine. You *read* books, you sexy thing. Literature really is our greatest gift, don't you think? So read, honey. Expand the mind. Parse the poetry and whatnot. Read it until its lines run through you like blood and its secrets are revealed."

"Asshole."

Silence descended upon them, and they walked on, Katharine obsessing over her endless questions, such that again she lost track of her surroundings, until they wordlessly turned down the Rue de Seine. Before she knew it, they were standing at the front entrance of her building, and Salt was saying this: "I can't help you anymore, Katharine. You're just going to have to fuck your way out of this one. I assume you realize that by now. So stop tormenting yourself with loose ends and enjoy the game."

"The game?"

"The game. The play. The seduction. The blowjob. The breasts. *Whatever. Enjoy* it. That's the point. It always has been the point and it always will be the point. And although I know I'll forever regret repeating something so ridiculously *mawkish*, I'll repeat it: don't worry about consequences, because whatever consequences there are, I personally promise not to let them be bad. So fuck, my dear. Fuck and read. Sound mind, sound body, et cetera."

At this a smile leapt to her face, her eyes shone with gratitude, and her lips kissed him hotly on the mouth. Salt pushed her gently away and glanced up to the lighted windows of the loft above. Then he strolled off, whistling merrily.

"Say hello to your boyfriend for me." he called out.

"Errr!" Katharine cried, gritting her teeth. Salt knew where she lived, and she'd been a fool, once again.

CHAPTER SEVEN

So she read the book. As Salt had suggested, she parsed its poetry and whatnot. And because she had done a lot of fucking, she did a lot of walking. She found other address clues in the pages of the Kama Sutra – positions she may have replicated – and then she attempted to find the addresses in real life. 187 Rue du Temple: on the page, missionary position, which wasn't exactly a help, and the address also happened to be a nondescript apartment building that gave her no further clues from the outside. 209 Boulevard Pasteur: a blowjob (just one man in the image) with the woman seated but bent over into the man's lap (that looked familiar and promising), but alas, not an address that existed, as far as Katharine could tell. At least not one she could find. So, 164 Rue de Provence: one woman giving cunnilingus to another, and also a brightly lit sushi place. She actually had a bite to eat there, so exhausted was she by the walking, but no mysterious stranger sidled over to ask if she would like to try some dessert. Taking the book from her purse, she hunched over it so as not to shock her fellow sushi eaters. The book may have been shocking to her when she had first obtained it, but now, she thought ruefully, it was like a scrapbook of memories. Ah, yes the White Lily. *Memories.* Flipping through the pages, she felt like a schizophrenic, torn between frustration and pride. Yep, she'd done that one too. 214 Avenue de la Bourdonnais, it looked like. Yes, it was going to be difficult to crack the next piece of the code when you considered the many positions she'd bent her body into over the past week.

Then she heard Nessim's voice saying: "Are you paying attention? Are you seeing yourself?" He had been trying to tell her something, and she flipped through the pages until she found it, right up front, page 102: a man lies on a floor, as flat as a desk. His hand presses down on the base of his cock so that it sticks straight up into the air. It is an enormous cock, far out of proportion with the man's body. And then, the Katharine figure in this scene: she is on all fours above the man – a brunette not a blonde – and she is lowering her crotch down towards the cock in an attempt to take it in. There are no words, no other obvious clues in the photo, but out the window rises Paris's only skyscraper, the Tour de Montparnasse, unmistakable as it sparkles in the sunlight. It's a stretch, but because Katharine knows now that the clues are there to be found, she finally feels certain of something: 102 Boulevard du Montparnasse.

Slamming the book shut, she left her sushi unfinished and caught a taxi. No consequences, no fear. This she repeated like a mantra.

The address was the site of a large bookstore. She walked in and began to browse the table of new releases, eyes darting back and forth in search of some other clue, something she could latch onto. Nothing appeared, no one appeared. Shoppers went on browsing the shelves, and nobody paid her any attention. She decided that she would ask for the manager. If the book was truly a code (and it *had* led her to Nessim), then it was a code all the time, not just at the moment she decided to appear on the scene. Meaning: her contact wouldn't be a shopper, but someone who could be there all the time. So the manager, she thought, ignoring the voice inside that said: *girl, you have lost your mind.*

The girl behind the information desk was far too high-strung to be mixed up in the secrets of the Kama Sutra, she decided. Her insistence on helping Katharine find just the right book was so friendly that it was almost frightening. *That girl,* Katharine thought, *needs to get fucked.* "Actually, I'd just like to speak to the manager," Katharine repeated.

"Is it a return?" the girl went on, desperate to please. "A question about one of our special offers?"

"Actually it's personal," Katharine snapped, and only after presenting another dozen happy options did the girl admit that the manager was currently absolutely unavailable. Alright then.

She would browse those damned books till closing, she would

parse the damned poetry, and if they shut off the lights and locked her inside, well she'd just keep browsing and parsing till dawn, or at least until someone made *something* clear. She browsed in art, but then she hated her job now and didn't want to think of art. Sex? Alright, sex. Over in the back corner there, although just a few minutes after her arrival in "Human Sexuality", she had decided that it was without a doubt the *least* sexy section of the store. Either you had a disease, or you might not get it up, or penis jokes made you snicker. For you overworked romantic types: *schedule* a sex date with your partner. "Then shoot yourself in the head," Katharine snarled, and subsequently slammed the book shut when she was advised to give her "partner" a particularly daring thrill by cooking dinner topless. Was it possible that Michel had been given this book years before and had made it his bible? Was it possible that his sexual identity, that sappy mix of cheap pride and cheaper feeling, had been obtained in the Human Sexuality section for nine euros and eighty cents? It was possible. That guy, Katharine thought, needs to get *fucked*.

Then she found herself almost in tears. She was just a fool wandering around Human Sexuality. She had to do something, but she seemed constitutionally incapable of ever figuring out what had to be done. She stared at the shelves in desperation. They would not help her, she knew, but as she stared, her eye fell along the spine of a book that was not done up in the awful pastels that the "experts" seemed to associate with sex. It was bound in leather, thin, and she slid it out of its spot. A Kama Sutra, funnily enough. Translated by Richard Burton, it said on the cover. She opened it up: an introduction, the philosophy of love and sex, and then finally the positions themselves. Beautiful photographs in this one too. More abstract than hers, but if possible, even more erotic because of that. She turned the pages and studied the photos closely, accustomed to looking for clues. But this book was properly numbered, and nothing stood out in the photos that might provide further information.

Until something did. It was the woman whom she recognized first. She was the deepest black, and more deeply beautiful than any woman Katharine had ever seen. Except that she had seen her before, in Hosnani's office, and her name was Neema. She was naked. She sat in the lap of a man, wrapping her impossibly long arms and legs around him. They were both in profile. The man sat on the floor and was fucking her that way. The man was Nessim. She turned the next page, then the next. More Nessim: clothed now, standing beside a desk with his cock in Katharine's mouth.

Horrified, Katharine flapped the book shut and shoved it into her purse with the other one. Nervously she glanced around the store. No one had seen her. Her heart was racing, and she breathed deeply in an attempt to calm herself down. Nessim! One thing she knew for certain now? She hated him more than all the rest.

So it was in this way that another fit of shoplifting came upon her. Typically she wouldn't have felt the need for another several months, and after the last time she had promised herself to give it up forever, but this was not typical. This was naked photos of herself available in one of Paris's most popular bookstores for just twenty five euros! Thankfully she was somewhat of a shoplifting expert. They wouldn't catch her. The last time had been a fluke. She was innocent looking: an American tourist in gay Paris. Innocent Katharine Bright, who loved to schedule sex with her "partner". Yes sir. She didn't look like a thief, that was for sure. Besides, the book was already in her bag. So just be your innocent, sunny self.

And it always gave her that thrill. Stealing cleared the mind and relieved stress. More precisely, it built up a stress so unbearable that when you had made it free and the stress was gone, it cleared out all of those little stresses along with it. Not that finding naked photos of herself in a bookstore was particularly little.

The buzzers were always the biggest hurdle. You could outwit cameras if you were careful (and innocent looking), but then of course you had to exit, and these days the threshold of almost every store was guarded by sensors that beeped if the corresponding sensor in whatever you carried hadn't been defanged by a cashier. But Katharine had stolen a book or two before (it was shameful, she knew), and they rarely had the chips inserted into them unless they were more expensive photo books. Which of course this Kama Sutra was, but she figured that it had only been in the store for a day or two at most, and so maybe they hadn't bothered to secure it. Also – and this thought frightened her – she realized that it was probably in her interest to get caught. Otherwise there was no guarantee that more photos of her wouldn't be on the shelves the next day.

So she steeled herself and stepped out onto the Boulevard du Montparnasse. Nothing sounded, nothing made a noise at all, and a rush of happiness overwhelmed her. She was free. Deeply she breathed in the night air, and she grinned. There was nothing she couldn't overcome with just a bit of grit.

She was still grinning when she felt a heavy hand on her shoulder and a deep voice saying (in English, strangely enough): "Madame, I'm afraid you'll need to come with me." The hand gripped her tighter. Terrified, she turned to face the voice. It was the mustachioed detective, the man who had bent her in two, still looking forbidding in his black suit and tie. She smiled feebly and said: "Thank god it's you."

The man who called himself a detective didn't smile back. It was as if he'd never set eyes on her before, much less come all over her belly. "I'm going to need to look in your bag," he said coldly, and before she could protest he had ripped the purse from her hands. Within seconds he had pulled the second Kama Sutra from the bag (leaving the first) and was waving it at her threateningly. "We've been looking for you," he snarled as a crowd began to gather. "We've had dozens of these disappear over the past few weeks. Sex books, all of them. It's disgusting."

With this he whipped a pair of handcuffs from his jacket pocket, spun her violently around, and snapped the cuffs onto her wrists, squeezing them till they hurt. Prodding her like a cow, he pushed her back into the store as dozens of appalled patrons looked on. *What kind of woman did such a thing?* Katharine had never been so embarrassed in her life, and she blushed violently. "Not that way," the man barked as she moved back into the store. "This way." Which was along the front wall of the store, through a swinging service door, and down a metal stairway. She was terrified, but at least she was saved from the crowd.

Pushing through another pair of double doors, they came into a basement stockroom filled with books on metal shelves and several large computers. Bare bulbs flickered dimly overhead, and the man instructed Katharine to stand still, then moved behind her and unlocked one of the cuffs. "*Thank you,*" she sighed. Then, furiously: "But did you really have to humiliate me like that?" The man didn't say a word. It was as if she hadn't spoken. He simply took her free wrist again, pulled her over to a bookshelf, and recuffed her to it.

"I see I'm in the right place!" she spat into his face. He just smiled, and walked around another shelf of books before disappearing. She rolled her eyes at nothing. Who would appear this time? She tugged at the handcuffs, but the shelves were full of books, and she wasn't going anywhere.

Five minutes passed, ten minutes. Then she heard movement again beyond the shelves, and the mustache appeared, followed by a young man in pink pants and a red Hawaiian shirt clashing so tremendously that she was almost put at ease. The man wasn't older than thirty, not particularly well-built, and fidgeting as if Katharine made him nervous. He snapped his fingers like a distracted twelve-year-old and hardly looked at her. Occasionally a hand darted up to his head to rake through his short, dark, unkempt hair. He wore unrimmed eyeglasses that made his eyes look unnaturally big. This was not a sex god, Katharine thought to herself, and that was an understatement.

"Switch Reno," he said off into the air, in a voice that had been Americanized but was still boyish and French. Katharine rolled her eyes again. She would just wait until the kid decided to translate that. "You're Katharine," he continued.

"That's right. Nice to know you've got the right girl locked up, isn't it. So who the hell are you?"

"Switch Reno," he said into the air again. The mustache stood beside him without moving a muscle.

"I'm sorry," Katharine said with a smirk. "*Switch?*"

"Computers. Integrated circuits. It's a nickname, it stuck. I made some money in tech, I'm retired from it now. Bought a few bookstores to put the money someplace."

"So let me guess. Now that you're retired, you *put people together.* You're a consultant of sorts. You make, sigh, *connections.*"

"I'll also make you shut up if you won't stand there and listen to what I have to say," he snapped, staring so intently at her that it was as if all of his haywire energy had been momentarily channeled into his eyes.

The eyes startled her, but she went on talking anyway: "Great. Then start with why I'm here."

He nodded a dozen quick times, looking down at her feet as if the answer might be there. "You have to go further, Katharine," he finally said. "You can't stop now."

"Fabulous. Unlock these cuffs, and I'll go far, far away. Cross my heart."

"Shut up," he said, fixing her again with that astonishingly confident stare. "Nobody asked you to come here. You came here on your own. So let's stop doing the damsel in distress act, and why don't you answer your own question for me. Why are you here?"

He was so focused on her now that she found herself wanting to give him an honest answer. She had been looking to get caught, and he was right: she could hardly complain. Why was she still pretending to be a detective? "Because I'm... a mystery to myself," she said suddenly. "I'm curious. I'm drawn to your group, whoever you are. I want to know more."

"You like sex."

Again her instinct was to make a crack and avoid the implications, but she forced herself to meet his eyes and said: "Okay, I like sex. I want to know more."

"Then listen to me," he said, stepping closer. "You are a pretty girl doing pretty things in pretty Paris. You are unknown. Solve the book and you will become one of *The Known*."

She didn't dare say anything now. Switch terrified her, he really did, but somehow it felt right that she should be terrified, and she did not want that feeling to go away just yet. "Good," he said, approving her submission. "Then let me tell you something more about our group. We call ourselves The Known. Informally – nobody prints it on a business card. I don't know how much you've studied Buddhism, but I was in Tibet for a while, long before I knew about The Known, and I became fascinated by Buddhist *recognitions*. When a lama dies - a Dalai Lama, for example - the elders scour the countryside looking for the boy that they recognize to be his reincarnation. This process can sometimes take years. Eventually, however, they see something in a boy. There is a certain power, or an uncanny wisdom. This is called a recognition, and the boy becomes the next lama, the next body to ferry that everlasting soul through a lifetime. I always found that so beautiful." He paused like a professor to gauge if she was following, but her face had become a mask.

"Alright. Now. Walk into a bar. Look across the room. You see him, or her, sitting there. Your eyes meet. Whether the person is beautiful or not, there is a pull so powerful that you cannot explain it even to yourself. This person could change your life. Katharine, this person *will* change your life if you just stand up and walk across that room. This has happened to you before. This has happened to everyone. But you don't walk across that room. You talk about nothing with your friends, you pretend to have a good time, you limit your glances, and then you leave. The next morning you've

forgotten the stranger. The next week, you've forgotten another one. The next year? You've forgotten how to look at all.
There are no longer life-changing strangers across the room,
because you no longer know how to see them. You recognize
nothing. You no longer even recognize yourself. Nights like
those, they always broke my heart. Do you understand what
I mean, Katharine."

"Yes," she whispered to the floor, so overwhelmed by the
force of the man's description that she could not bear to look
at him now.

"It is terrible, isn't it?" he said softly. "But imagine this. Imagine learning to see again. Imagine remembering how to live
again. Imagine recognizing that possibility in the faces of
others. And then imagine that there are others who have
learned this for themselves, and who will be across that
room, meeting your eyes. They will know what you know,
because they have learned it again too. Sex is just the eventual
manifestation of that moment. Real sex is the ultimate recognition of the worth of another. Eyes locked in the bedroom
are the most powerful force in the world, more than atomic
energy, more than the biggest hurricane. The barriers come
down, and you become something vastly more than you ever
dreamed you could be. You become angels, monsters, super-
heroes, geniuses, gods. You have to dare risking your everything, but for those few who can do that, the reward is the

world's everything. I believe this, Katharine. I know it. But you have to be open to it first. You have to recognize the others first. And once the barrier of the ordinary is finally destroyed, the possibilities are infinite."

"How do I do that?" she murmured.

"There a several hundred of us in Paris, thousands in the world. We see each other in an organized way from time to time. We fuck, we discover uncharted territory. But most of the time we're out in the world, in that imaginary bar, looking for a recognition, looking for someone who sees what we see and is willing to put their bodies on the line in the service of some undiscovered glory. Fucking, Katharine. You don't know the half of it. So join us."

"*How?*" she cried, entranced by his words and longing for those glories. "*Recognize* me. Please."

"You are here because we see you across the room," he said, his eyes locked commandingly on hers. "The question is whether you'll stop pretending to be the woman you've always pretended to be. If you truly believed in that old Katharine, you wouldn't be here. Most people live happily enough by believing in their definition of themselves. We don't bother with them. But you do not believe in your definition, and that's the answer to why you came here tonight. The new question is whether you'll go far enough to escape it."

He had moved even closer as he spoke, and now their faces almost touched. "Do it to me," she whispered into his mouth, forcing herself to look into his wild eyes. She wondered if she was falling in love – no, it wasn't love, at least not the way she had felt it before, but it was equally overpowering and emotional.

"Do it to me," she whispered again, and in one quick move-ment Switch ripped her blouse down the front. "Toto, get the camera," he said, and the man apparently named Toto disappeared again, passing Switch the keys to the cuffs as he went. Then to Katharine: "I want to keep you motivated. No-body else will see it. Amateur videography is just a passion of mine."

She was helpless to defend herself. Not that she wanted to defend herself as Switch closed the gap between them and kissed her. Although her hands were cuffed to a bookshelf, in the basement of a bookstore, she eagerly kissed him back, and it felt like, well, just like a wonderful, gooey kiss. Then he ripped her skirt from her waist, popping its button. She stepped out of the skirt as he gently slid her panties away. "We'll leave the heels on," he said, as he pressed into her again and reached around to unsnap her bra. It was naked then, that glorious body of hers, and Switch pressed into it harder.

Their tongues locked passionately, and she felt his hands at her wrists, fumbling at the lock of the cuffs. She wanted to throw her arms around his neck, but once he'd cleared a hand, he didn't let her go. He pulled the blouse and the bra from the freed hand, then locked his hands around her wrists as tightly as the cuffs and raised her arms above her head until he found another edge of the bookshelf on which he could fasten her. She bared her teeth into his mouth as he clasped the cuffs even tighter. "Now turn around," he said, stepping back abruptly. So she did, feeling the twist of the cuffs at her wrist. She showed him her ass, that perfect pale construction, and in her captured desire she even thrust it out towards him as far as she could make it go before the cuffs limited her display. Switch drew back a hand and slapped her ass as hard as he possibly could. She bucked against the shelves and groaned: "Is that all you got?"

Meanwhile Toto had set up a video camera on a tripod and had moved closer to observe. "Your turn, Toto," Switch said, and so Toto stepped up, like a batter to the plate, and slapped her too. She braced herself and took the blow. Her hips hardly moved, and her ass still jutted out like a proud challenge. She was hanging from the cuffs now, all of her weight at her wrists, but that pain was negligible compared to the pleasure of defying these men with her perfect ass. Looking under her arm, defiant and lusty, she saw Switch take position behind her again, but instead of hitting her, he reached out a hand to gently cup her pussy, which was already sopping in anticipation. "Just hit me again, Switch," she grunted, but he did not take his hand from her cunt.

His thumb, however, had begun to explore. It pressed at her virgin anus as his fingers tickled her labia. The sensation momentarily caused her to lose the thread and observe the scene from a distance. The thumb scared her there. No one had ever entered her that way, and the consequences of crossing that dark portal made her unusually uncomfortable. Switch, however, was obviously quite comfortable with the gesture, and before she could cry out in protest, his thumb had slipped past the pale, pink dimple that she had never associated with sex, sending shivers of pleasure all the way up her spine until it tickled the hairs at the back of her neck. When she didn't protest, he moved his thumb in further, further, until she felt the web of his fingers at her electrified perineum and shrieked her unqualified assent. Switch then reached around her and began to fondle her hanging breasts as his thumb moved smoothly in and out of her anus. She had expected the act to unloose an embarrassing cascade, but no, it was just glorious, and she was clean and sexy and maddeningly horny. Toto then pressed into her side and took a breast for himself, and then she was kissing him, thirstily, wanting these two men to do with her whatever they wished. Whatever, wherever. Just do it to me, and don't tell me about it in advance.

She swayed out to meet Switch's thumb as Toto lowered his mouth to suck at a nipple, and she thrust out her chest to smother that too, feeling the tantalizing prickle of his mustache at her areole. She wished her hands were free to fondle their crotches and make them hard, as mad with lust as she now was, but it was thrilling to be controlled in this way too, and she soon discovered that their lust needed no assistant. As he licked her nipple, Toto's hard cock pressed through his pants against her thigh. She saw it in her mind, hooded, uncircumcised. She saw it in her mouth and groaned. Then Switch's dick too, pressed into the hard line of flesh between her cheeks. As his thumb continued fucking her, she felt his other hand fumbling with his zipper, and then it was hard flesh pressing against hard flesh. She could feel everything. There must have been a dozen couples fucking within a mile radius, and she could feel them all, as if their flesh was hers.

Then Switch removed his thumb. Fingers entered her pussy, and she rose up on her toes with pleasure, heels spiked backwards. She was still astonished to discover that there was a whole new part of her body that had been asleep forever, but that had now been brought to life. Her anus felt like another pussy, strangely aware of the pleasures that could be bestowed upon it, and straining towards them now. Switch let his cock slide over it again and again, teasing that new pink kiss. She groaned as Toto's pants dropped to the floor, and she felt the hard slab of his flesh now at her knee, rubbing up and down to the same beat as Switch. Crouching, Toto had shifted around to the front of her so that he could lick both breasts, which he jiggled in his hands.

Then she felt herself begin to split. She felt a hot nub of flesh press up into her asshole and she feared she would tear. Jerking at the handcuffs, she cried out in pain. Switch was not interested in her pain. He pressed into her further, and she screamed. Then further, still gently, and it didn't hurt so much anymore. Then further, and she groaned, a dark, guttural cry that she had never before heard from her mouth. Further: his cock was fully inside her now, and it was easy. The pain was gone, and surprisingly that hole was as smoothly lubricated as her pussy. Another virginity was gone, and she wondered how many others there might be.

And the *sensation!* She could feel every single bit of that cock, every slight movement back and forth, much more than she could ever feel in her dumb, swamped pussy (her wonderful, dumb pussy, of course, but this was different, and this was marvelous). Slowly, building up steam, Switch began to fuck up into her ass with long, regular strokes, and she loved it, every inch of it, and she hung by the cuffs to get even closer to him.

Then Toto unlocked the cuffs, and she slumped down over the bookshelf, sideways so that she caught herself from the floor with her hands. Switch managed to keep inside of her by staying deep and pivoting around her. Once she was settled on hands and knees, her bent body had brought him even deeper, and she loved it, she wanted it. In the anus it could not go too deep. There was no limit. There was only deeper. So she pressed back against him and drove that cock further in. The rhythm recommenced, and she shrieked with pleasure. She shrieked right into Toto's cock, which he had quickly positioned in front of her face. Like a snake, she licked at it.

"I thought you didn't do that," Toto growled.

"Last week," she whispered, grabbing the uncircumcised flesh with her hand and stroking it vigorously. "Last week I didn't do that, Toto." Then she was taking it deep into her mouth as Switch gave it to her deep from behind. She growled and spat and sighed, caught between cocks in a way she could never have conceived. She put both hands to the floor to press harder against Switch. She fucked Toto's cock with her mouth, trusting him to control his thrusts. Forward, her lips straining towards the base of Toto's cock, backwards, lunging to take all of Switch's cock into that dark and crackling passage. The men stood like stone statues as she shifted back and forth between them, controlling the rhythm. For a moment she supported herself on one hand in order to paw at her drenched slit, but she could not take it – not the weight of her body (she was in such good dancing shape that she could have supported it for days), but the additional sensation. More pleasure and she would explode, and within minutes she had. Despite her intense pleasure, the orgasm astonished her when it came. Her pussy was untouched, and yet fireworks exploded through it just the same, just from the pleasure she had taken from Switch's cock in her other hole. He came as she did, pulling out to splash her ass with come as she wiggled it enticingly. Toto came too, but she would not let him splash his drop. She wanted to know his taste too, to learn the different vintages of come like a sommelier of men. He was saltier than Nessim, and she almost gagged, but she almost came again too, so exciting it was to think of herself sucking down semen like that. Then they all collapsed in a heap with a communal groan.

Later she dressed and walked out into the night, wearing Switch's Hawaiian shirt. She had left her tattered bra and underwear behind, but she immediately realized that she would no longer feel the same kick she once had in strolling down the sidewalk naked underneath. That was just a dare, a silly game that had been fun to play, but this was a complete reconfiguration. She felt as if she had been transformed. She felt no fear. She could taste the stars on her tongue. She wanted to roar up at the sky. She wanted to lick the night and wound it with her teeth.

She wanted to *know*.

CHAPTER EIGHT

Harriet had obviously decorated her own apartment in the Marais. It was all black and white, with angular couches and slashing art on the walls. Harriet herself sat on a black leather couch wearing a black silk shirt unbuttoned halfway down her chest and a short, tight black skirt, underneath which she had folded her tanned legs. Katharine sat on the other end of the couch, looking as if she had been decorated by Harriet too. Her skirt was black and just as short, and she had kicked off her shoes to curl up on the couch as well. Her shirt was silk and black too. They had laughed about it when she arrived, just half an hour after calling. They had undone another shirt button and had laughed about that too.

"The society exists, Katharine," Harriet was saying over a glass of red wine. "I can have indescribable sex every night of the week, without boring myself with the empty formalities I used to have to perform to get into bed. There are others who think like me, and most nights I'll see one of them. Or two."

"Women? I mean, are you a lesbian?"

"Boring," Harriet sighed, then took Katharine's hand and continued. "Sex is the biggest thing in the world, Katharine. Sometimes I think it's the only thing. For me, at least, I know it is. Once you know that and admit it, the rest becomes easy." She glanced up at Katharine again and looked amused by what she saw: "Poor Katharine!" she cried sympathetically, kissing her hand. "You're all worked up again, aren't you? Can't I help?"

"Please!" Katharine said, and then Harriet was wrapping her arms around her, kissing her deeply. Occasionally Harriet would draw back with glittering eyes and moistened lips to look at her. Each time Katharine felt herself waiting in a frenzy of anticipation for what might happen next. Harriet tossed back her head and laughed, then removed her shirt and let it fall to the floor. Her skirt came off then, and she was not wearing bra or underwear. She rose to stand before Katharine, stark naked and supreme.

"Now you too," she hissed to Katharine. "Strip! Go on! Every stitch. Take it off!" Katharine found herself obeying. She could not resist Harriet, and she could not resist herself. She fumbled at zippers and buttons and let her clothes fall to the floor. She unleashed her fabulous breasts, then wriggled daintily out of her panties, and finally she stood there naked too, every bit as statuesque as Harriet. Stabs of desire shot through her, and she visibly shivered, waiting again for what might happen next. Harriet faced her now, her fingers violently lashing at her own nipples, desire beginning to cloud her face. The sight of Katharine's now naked body only seemed to torment her more.

Then she swiftly crossed to a cupboard and removed an object from it. This she held out to Katharine: a short-handled whip with a head of many leather lashes knotted at the end. Katharine took the whip, feeling its weight in her hand, tentatively touching the lashes, which were about a foot long. The tight leather knots were as hard as pebbles.

"Now!" Harriet said. "You'll whip me with this. I want you to whip me all over – my back, my buttocks, even my tits. If I tell you to whip harder, I want you to whip harder – all over, even across my pussy if you can. I'll scream, but don't stop. Just whip and keep whipping!"

With this she stepped over to the couch and lay on her back, quivering in the grip of some strange obsession. Katharine watched in astonishment, the whip held limply by her side.

"Now!" Harriet commanded, cupping her breasts in her hands, fondling them, offering them up as a sacrifice to Katharine, who sighed and let the lashes fall once, lightly, across the skin.

"Not like that!" Harriet shouted. "Harder! Hard as you can, be merciless! Draw blood if you can!" And suddenly Katharine, now completely coupled to the other woman's will, seemed to accept her strange role. She raised the whip and flicked the lashes across the nipples presented by Harriet's hands. Harriet winced as the whip stung her flesh, and her nipples hardened further as Katharine raised the whip again. Once more Katharine let her arm drop. Again and again she raised her arm, and again and again she lashed at the breasts of the woman who now wriggled in agony beneath the onslaught.

As if by instinct, Katharine then switched her attack to the belly and thighs of the writhing body on the couch. She was so focused on her savage task that she did not even hear the moans that her torture provoked. She reached out her free hand and grabbed Harriet's hair. She used the hair to wrench the woman around, so that her perfect buttocks were exposed. Then she attacked the ass, blindly, violently, raining down blows upon the tanned flesh, which was soon stained red. She stared in fascination as Harriet, sobbing from the pain, wriggled up to squat on her knees and jut her ass into the air.

"Strike!" she howled. "Harder! Mutilate me! For fuck's sake, don't stop now. I'm going to come! Any moment now I'll come!" The fleshy spheres presented to Katharine were now an angry, inflamed red. In some places blood even appeared near the surface. But they were like magnets, those buttocks, to the rising and falling whip. Again and again it descended. And then Harriet, utterly consumed by the agony, did a terrible thing. Moving her arms back down to the seat of the couch and arching her back, she attempted to fold her torso back through her thighs in order to fully expose the mound of her cunt from reverse. The way she knelt, ass in the air, all that seemed visible between the swells of her ass was her bare and gleaming cunt, just below the pinched circle of her anus.

Katharine thrashed it with the whip, fiercely hypnotized by the way Harriet's cunt seemed to strain towards each stroke. Only a few minutes had passed since the whipping had begun, but it seemed like hours. Suddenly Harriet's legs shot out, kicking straight back so that her belly crashed onto the couch, and Katharine sensed that an orgasm was close. Sweating from her exertions, Katharine's skin gleamed in the light, but she did not stop the whipping. Up and down it went, now across Harriet's twisting back again. The howls of the tortured woman as her orgasm split the pain were horrifying.

Then Katharine could whip no more. Her arm refused to raise itself. She let it hang as if it was wounded, and the whip fell from her fingers. Then she fell too, fainting sharply to the floor. On the couch above, Harriet's body was still racked by the aftershocks of her terrible pleasure. She was simultaneously consumed by the hell of pain and the heaven of an extraordinary rapture.

The sound of running water accompanied Katharine's return to consciousness. Then Harriet was bent over her, wiping her forehead with a cool, moist towel. Katharine groggily shook her head, adjusting to her surroundings again, to her own naked body and that of the woman hovering above her. She mechanically answered Harriet's sympathetic questions. Everything felt strange, but strangest of all was the tense coil in her groin - the heaviness there, frustration pressing down. Numbly she struggled to her feet.

"Poor girl," Harriet fussed. "Come with me. A bath will do you good." Katharine took the woman's arm and let herself be led to the bathroom, where water already steamed in the tub. The bath was big enough for both of them, and they slid into the water, fitting themselves to its porcelain curves. Soon Katharine felt herself reviving in the warm water. She began to notice things again. The bathroom: its mirrors, its towels, its luxurious fittings. Then Harriet: she cringed at the sight of the red lashes across the woman's beautiful breasts. She closed her eyes and cringed at the memory of her part in mutilating that splendid body.

"Doesn't it hurt?" she asked, eyes slowly opening.

"Terribly, darling," Harriet murmured. "But wonderfully. And you! You were just fabulous."

"No. I don't know what got into me. I don't know how…how I could have been like that. How could I have done that to you?"

"Please, Katharine. You did beautifully. You were perfect."

"But Harriet, those marks! How can you stand it?"

"Acquired taste, darling. Maybe you'll acquire it one day too."

"The first time must have been so frightening."

"Frightening? I don't know. I don't remember, really. It was such a long time ago."

"Tell me about it."

Harriet gently laved her arms and breasts with a soapy cloth and said: "Seven or eight years ago, I had just discovered the group – or they had discovered me. I had gone to a chateau outside of Paris with another woman especially for the experience, at her invitation. She was a lot like I am now, I guess. Incredibly experienced. At the time, though, much of this was still a big mystery to me. Anyway. From her I learned what I had gone to learn."

"Well I would have been terrified."

"I guess I was too. But it was something I felt compelled to do. I had to go through with it, to find out what it was all about. I can't even explain it, Katharine…."

"Do…do you think it would work with me?"

Harriet laughed: "Honestly, I don't. Sex is so particular, after all. You're enjoying the experimenting, it seems clear to me, but that kind of thing is a dangerous experiment. It can easily go wrong. So I'd say you would have to feel that compulsion too, to feel a genuine hunger for the experience. If you do, then of course you have to go for it. But you're not like me."

After a moment Harriet went on reminiscing: "She was pure sex, that woman. It exuded from her, and although he had done absolutely *everything*, she was never, ever vulgar."

"My kind of girl," Katharine said with a smile.

"Yes she was," Harriet said, smiling too. Then Katharine bit her lip and thought for a moment. She had come with so many questions for Harriet, but somehow their astonishing experiment had removed all questions but one: "What do I do next, Harriet?"

"Oh darling," Harriet cried sympathetically. "You're doing so wonderfully. I've so much enjoyed our times together. But if you're talking about the group and your place in it, then I'll say just one thing: you have to get out of the book."

Katharine was tempted to ask more, but she knew from

Harriet's tone that their conversation was done. They toweled each other off. Harriet eased into a bathrobe, Katharine dressed again, and after a lingering kiss beside the front door, she went out into the night.

Get out of the book? she thought to herself as she walked past the buzzing cafes on the Rue Vieille du Temple. What did that mean? Throw it away? Forget the whole thing? Invent new positions (as if that whipping hadn't been kinky enough)? It was another riddle to be deciphered, but she was too tired for more riddles, and so she got out of the book, at least for a while, by simply putting it out of her mind.

CHAPTER NINE

Arnaud's girlfriend had broken up with him, and he couldn't believe it. Sitting on the edge of Katharine's desk, his face expressed pure astonishment as he talked, and talked, trying to come to terms with those unfamiliar things called emotions. Of course his girlfriend loved him in her "heart of hearts", he told Katharine. She was just going through a "woman thing", but he couldn't bear the thought of "living so alone", and he had to admit that his "soul hurt". Katharine made a mental note never to trust a man who could be so saccharine. Sugar was something you added to a cake, not the cake itself.

And Katharine had work to do. She was thoroughly fed up with Arnaud's soul, but she found herself taking pity on him all the same. He simply had no idea. So she kept nodding and murmuring vague words of support. Hey, surely they could work something out. Love, you know.

"Will you come have a quick coffee with me?" he begged with misty eyes. "I just can't be alone right now."

Ugh. "Alright," she sighed, and over espressos downstairs she kept doing her best to console the guy. It was a difficult moment, sure, but he had to look on the bright side. Take her, for example: recently this whole Nicolas thing had been stressing her out. Not knowing where he was. Not being able to do her work. Not being able to talk about it. But she just kept trying to stay positive.

"Wait," Arnaud said sharply, breaking through his fog of self-pity. "This Nicolas thing?"

"Yeah," Katharine said, her voice still soft and reassuring. "The personal problems that have kept him from work. You probably know more about it than me."

"*Nicolas?*" Arnaud asked again, the old grin creeping onto his face. "*Personal problems?* He's in Saint Bart's, Katharine. Ha! He always spends a week there this time of year. Probably fucks the entire island, the bastard, and then on the seventh day he rests."

"Not this year, Arnaud," she said with a touch of uncertainty. "Other things happened that, well..."

"Katharine!" he interrupted, really enjoying himself now, loving the spectacle of her stupidity. "I talked to him *yesterday* about the Malvaux sale! Jesus!" Laughter shook him, and he had to put a hand to his mouth to keep from spitting out coffee. "You're really in love with him, aren't you? It's...so... *sweet!* Ha!"

"Fuck you, Arnaud," Katharine snarled, utterly bewildered by the news, and furious about that. "Fuck you and your sob story. If that girlfriend of yours has any kind of sense, she'll never let you *near* her again."

But Arnaud hardly heard the jab. He had found the way to restore himself at the center of his own universe. He was Arnaud again. "He doesn't care about you," he cooed. "I've seen research assistants come and go, but you've stayed the longest, and you want to know why? You know what saves you? You're too frigid to let him into your pants. Come *on*, Katharine. You've got to *loosen up.*"

He touched her arm as he said this. She swatted it away like a fly, eyes shooting fire, mouth twisted in hatred. Arnaud just went on grinning, fully expecting her to innocently swoon into his arms after his "sensitive" morning confessions, so she stepped up to him until their faces were just a foot apart, looked down on him from her additional two inches of height, and said: "Frigid? *Frigid?!* Arnaud, you will always be wrong about women – and I mean every woman you set eyes upon from now until your lonely death. Frigid? I shave my pussy, and I let strange women lick it. I fuck dildos the size of your pitiful arms. Yeah, I'm frigid. I suck cocks in movie theaters with these cock-sucking lips of mine, and I don't let men go. I love the taste of their come shooting into my mouth. I take it in the ass. Have you ever taken it in the ass, Arnaud? Well I just love it, and if it ever is something you find yourself wanting to try, I would recommend sucking a cock at the same time. I like to be spit-roasted, Arnaud. And I whip people. Just a couple of nights ago I whipped a woman until she bled, because the *frigid* bitch was just begging for it. I whipped her tits, and I whipped her cunt, and I loved it so much that my pussy just dripped. Do you like whipping, Arnaud? Do you want me to whip that puny little dick of yours? No?"

Arnaud had gone stark pale. All expression was leeched from his face as he watched her tirade in dumb horror. For a moment he looked as if he was searching for something to say. Then he hung his head, turned, and walked out of the café.

"How about a Pernod," Katharine said to the bartender. When he set it down, she drank it quickly and strode out of the café with a triumphant grin on her face. Back in the office she discovered that Arnaud had immediately gone home sick, and she decided to leave too.

Michel came home a couple of hours later. "Hey," he said as he walked in. "Hey," she said, and he disappeared to the bedroom to work at his desk. She lay on the couch looking up at the ceiling and wondering how one was meant to "get out of the book". This thought preoccupied her for hours. Outside the sun set, the moon rose, and traffic roared then died out again. It was almost midnight when the phone rang. She leapt to pick it up. It was Salt, and he'd heard from Anita. She was supposed to meet him later on, and if Katharine was still interested, then she was welcome to come along.

"Where?" Katharine asked.

"Porte Dauphine. The Allée des Poteaux, just at the entrance of the Bois de Boulogne. Selena and I are heading there now."

"I'm on my way."

"Alright then. And Katharine? Wear a skirt."

"What?"

"See you soon." She wanted to ask more, but Salt had hung up. Nevermind. This was finally it, and her heart raced with excitement. So…a skirt. That meant the bedroom, of course, and Michel would just have to deal with it. Ignoring him completely, she rushed into her closet and began to change. He ignored her at first, pretending to be utterly captivated by financial statements or whatever they were, but soon he realized that Katharine might not just be preparing for bed, and he turned to give her an exasperated look. "What the hell are you doing?"

"I have to go see some friends," she said breathlessly.

"At midnight? What the hell is *wrong* with you?"

"Whatever it is, darling," she said lightly, "it's nothing compared to what's wrong with you." Checking herself in the mirror and nodding her approval, she moved for the bedroom
door. Michel leapt from his chair and caught her arm. "You're
not going anywhere at this time of night," he growled. So she
kicked him in the shin and ran. As he groaned and doubled
over in pain, she ripped open the front door to flee into the
night. "*You tell me where you're going!*"

Down on the Rue de Seine, she looked around frantically for
a taxi, but the streets were quiet and so she ran towards the
Boulevard Saint Germain, glancing over her shoulder every
few steps to see if Michel was in pursuit. On her third or
fourth glance he appeared, charging like a bull. "Taxi!" she
desperately cried. Finally one appeared, and she lunged out
onto the asphalt to snatch open its door. As she slammed
it shut, Michel appeared at the window, shouting something
she couldn't hear. Then the driver accelerated away, and she
was safe. Her head fell back on the seat in relief. After a moment the driver asked where they were going, and she told
him. "The Bois de Boulogne?" he asked, eyes questioning her

in the rearview mirror. "Drive," she said. Behind her out the window, Michel was waving to an empty street.

At the Porte Dauphine she got out and asked the driver to point her towards the Allée des Poteaux. He reluctantly nodded off to the left, and then he abandoned her to walk into the woods alone. She had only taken a dozen steps when another taxi screeched up and Michel tumbled out. He barked something at the driver and called after her, but she just kept walking. Hesitating for a moment, he then threw some money into the taxi and set off in pursuit of her. "Katharine!" he cried out, as her eyes nervously scanned the darkened wood, desperate for Salt to appear.

Then Michel was at her side, grabbing her arm again, which she snatched away. Unable to physically restrain her (she'd like to see him try), he decided to appeal to her good sense: "Katharine! You don't know what you're doing. These *cannot* be friends of yours. The Bois de Boulogne? Do you know what this place is? This is a place for *putes*, for prostitutes. It is famous for it. This is where they come at night, and men take them into the woods. Gays, too. This is where they all come. The filthiest people come to the Bois de Boulogne, Katharine. Transsexuals. Terrible things happen here. You are not safe!" And then, as if to confirm his fear, there was a noise in the bushes beside them, and they both stopped in their tracks. When the sound didn't come again, Katharine walked on, but soon they could see painted women lingering around the sparse streetlamps, and then off through the trees, forms moving on top of other forms and the grunt of men locked in quick fucks with other men. She could tell that Michel was not only furious, but scared. "Let me take you home," he pleaded, and so she turned to him and delivered her ultimatum: "Michel, I don't want you here. But if you insist on following me, then shut up and do what I say. Otherwise just leave right now. Understand?"

He nodded grudgingly, with hatred in his eyes, and they walked on. "You're being crazy," he murmured.

"You have no idea how crazy. Now shut up or I'll find someone to shut you up. I'll scream, and they will hurt you."

A few hundred meters into the park, Salt and Selena appeared, he in blue jeans and the standard black t-shirt, she in fluorescent mini everything, such that she could have been another of the woman who lingered under the lamps with their hips thrust out. "Where is she?" Katharine asked, kissing them both on the cheeks.

"You're no fun," Selena purred, grabbing Katharine's hand and shoving it up under her own skirt. Selena wasn't wearing underwear and was already wet with anticipation – for whatever was meant to come next.

"She'll be here," Salt said wryly. "You don't find Anita by looking, though. She's the type that only replies to a mating call." Then nodding at Michel: "Boyfriend's not saying much."

"He's been given orders."

"You sure you want to do this?"

"He insisted upon it. I don't want him here, but maybe it will be educational. It's his fucking choice." She thought of her morning speech to Arnaud. She thought of giving the same speech to Michel right then and there, but then maybe she needed to find a way to actually demonstrate what she'd become and be done with their stupid charade. Maybe she had loved him – that was a generous thought – but she didn't anymore.

"Alright then," Salt said gaily. "There are two paths in the woods. We take the one less traveled by." With this he jauntily led them off the path and across a grassy field, like a scout master leading his charges off on a wilderness adventure. She half expected him to break out into a peppy call-and-response and wait for them to echo back.

They crossed the field and pushed through a hedge. Michel cursed under his breath, and Katharine silenced him with a glance. She had no idea where they were going, although she assumed the final destination was sex, but strangely enough, she trusted Salt, and despite the anchor of Michel at her side, she realized that she was actually getting a kick out of the adventure. She loved the mystery of it, and she was willing to let it stay a mystery until it wasn't anymore.

They walked down another path and then off again through a grove of trees, where Salt stopped and said: "Here we are." Michel snorted, but Katharine was done with him. She was looking off into the shadows, and there were bodies moving out there. Selena immediately scampered off until she was just another dark body. "You *really* sure you want to do this?" Katharine heard Salt ask. She didn't answer. She had already set off after Selena, into the shadows where the dark forms became more and more detailed until she saw that there were a couple dozen bodies spread over a large area of grass, all naked, most fucking, some just riveted spectators. Katharine was riveted too – men fucking men and women who were fucking men and women, bodies coupled in every way imaginable, but even the most strained poses looked beautiful. Katharine thought fleetingly of her realization while stalking through the streets the week before: beauty could be found in anyone if you knew how to look. Of course many of the bodies were absolutely stunning, and Katharine watched them with a sort of reverence, but the less obviously beautiful bodies drew her just as completely – for their vitality and the incredible capacity they had for finding and taking pleasure. Sex had stripped everyone of all pretension, and it was beautiful out there.

"Is it always like this?" Katharine asked in wonder.

"No," Selena said, as enthralled by the scene as Katharine, "but sometimes a message goes out, and we come. Oh, I'm so excited! Kiss me, Katharine." And so Katharine leaned down to kiss the woman, gently at first, then passionately. Selena was a hot little number, and Katharine immediately understood why she had been asked to wear a skirt. Selena had her hand up between Katharine's legs in a flash. She was so consumed by the kisses that it took her a while to realize that her panties had magically disappeared. Selena was a magician and had her dripping wet with astonishing speed. Katharine's hand reached out to reciprocate, and they stood like that for a while, lasciviously kissing with their arms crossing towards each other's cunts. Around them in the darkness bodies were being stripped and pulled to the grass. Katharine looked on excitedly as she kissed, telling herself a thousand times that this, yes, was an actual orgy. If at first she had also been watching for an appearance of Anita, she quickly forgot about that. Selena had unbuttoned her shirt to lick at her breasts, and then there was an unknown man behind her kissing her neck, and hands at the zipper of her skirt, and she was going down, down, down, letting herself be kissed all over with her bare back against the cool grass.

Never had there been such a wonderful experience as this. *This is so wonderful,* she kept thinking. It was the only thought her mind could formulate, because her body was overwhelmed with sensations, and there were delicious people everywhere moving to and fro. She held onto some as they passed, and others held onto her. Orgasms came and went like the tides. At one moment she opened her eyes to discover that she was kissing a rugged, hairy man and there was a couple – a man and woman – both licking at her pussy. Selena was gone, Salt was holding someone against a tree trunk, and Michel had blessedly disappeared. Thank god. For a moment there she'd feared he would fight for her honor. And only an idiot could fail to see how honorable it was to have your pussy double licked by such an attractive couple.

Was it inevitable that she eventually found herself in the arms of Salt? He made her laugh, and she wanted to kiss him. She also liked his smell, his confidence ..his cock. "You've never actually fucked me, have you?" she sighed as his hands tightly gripped her ass to pull her into his naked bulk.

"God you're sexy," he groaned.

"Put it in me, John," she whispered, grinding up against him. "Put it in me now." With this he swept her up, lightly laid her on the grass, and was on her in an instant. She sighed and spread her legs out wide. He felt so good. Everything felt so wonderful.

She fucked with her eyes open because there was so much

to see, so many naked bodies stalking after pleasure like prehistoric hunters. Just beside them two men were fucking, paralleling her missionary style with Salt, and she watched in fascination as their sleek, muscled bodies grappled and bucked. She was entranced by the muscled buttocks of the man on top, who was driving his large cock into the buttocks of the other, who frantically stroked his own throbbing cock with his legs held in the air. She was fascinated by the grimaces on their faces and their masculine kisses. She wished she had a cock, and as Salt steadily fucked her, she reached out a hand to feel the muscular slab of chest on the man laid out on the ground. He was delicious, and god, she wished she had a cock. He took her hand and began to gently kiss it as the cock of his lover drove into him. Salt, as attentive and experienced as he was, saw the shifting of her desire and without taking his masterful cock from her depths, he wrenched her around until the two pairs formed a V and her mouth was close to the man's. Swinging one leg over Salt's head like a chorus girl, so that she lay on her side with Salt's cock now entering her sideways and from behind, she kissed the man deeply, feeling the rough stubble of his beard on her face. She gave him all of her tongue, her hand roving around his solid chest and smooth, hard belly. She moaned into his ear – the new position let her feel Salt even better – and then kissed him and kissed him again. After a while she noticed that a new figure had joined them. It was Michel, standing above them still fully clothed with a mixture of fascination and horror on his face.

He looked as if he had been prepared to say something definitive, but the sight of Katharine and these men had struck him dumb. And yet he still didn't turn away, she thought with satisfaction, as she took her neighbors cock in her hand and emitted a loud groan.

"Join us, Michel," she said coyly, her voice jumping with Salt's every stroke. Michel looked down on her with hatred and methodically began to unbutton his shirt. "Ooh, Michel!" she mocked, her head lolling on the grass now as Salt slammed into her. "Aren't you daring!"

Michel flung his shirt to the ground, bent to clumsily slip out of his shoes, then resolutely unzipped his pants, gritting his teeth at Katharine as he did. "Och, teach us a lesson," she cooed, turning to kiss the impaled man beside her again. This left Michel standing there foolishly in his oversized boxer shorts, as if he had expected his strip to bring Katharine to her senses. "I'm afraid I'm a bit occupied," she said, pulling Salt's face down towards hers to kiss him deeply, then turning to kiss her neighbor, then Salt again, their faces so close that they all could have kissed. "But do show my friends that cock of yours."

With this Michel furiously ripped the boxers from his waist and petulantly stomped them down to the ground, thus revealing what had shamed him even more than his nudity. His cock stood straight out, throbbing with need. Despite all of his outrage, Katharine's debauchment had excited him. His cock had betrayed him, and he looked down on it bewilderedly. "You like to see me fucked, don't you Michel?" she purred between kisses. Thumbing her own nipples, she said: "You like those cocks in me, don't you? Well come over here. Come between us." As Michel took a terrified step forward, she lifted herself up on an arm until she could roll up onto Salt so that his back was on the ground now and she was sitting on his cock, facing the beautiful man with the fabulous ass who was still driving into her former neighbor, face clenched as he miraculously struggled against an overdue release.

"Come here, Michel," she said, and he took another step forward so that she could take him in her mouth. She had never done this to him before, and she wanted to show him just what she knew, so she took him deep, deeper, until her lips were at his balls. She had never seen him so hard, and his pubic hair reeked of desire.

After that one deep thrust, however, she left him and kissed the beautiful man again, and with the kiss she led the man's mouth back to Michel. She sucked Michel's cock, and then she kissed the man. She licked the base of Michel's shaft as the man's eyes watched ravenously, and then she drew back again, and nodded, and the man began to suck as she looked on in fascination, still grinding slowly on top of Salt. Michel had his eyes closed and was making faint animal sounds. She wondered whether he assumed it was still her mouth at his dick, or whether he had decided to pretend that it was. Devilishly, she decided to find out. As the man went on sucking, taking it expertly into the depths of his mouth in a way she never could have managed, she began to lick Michel's balls – lightly at first, so that he might think he was imagining it, then smothering the balls with the flat of her tongue. A groan caught in Michel's throat, and his eyes snapped open. "God that turns me on," she whispered up to him, and she had never seen such an awful moment of struggle on a man's face. Then something clicked. He hated her, he hated himself, but his dick was throbbing, and he was going to let it be sucked.

Grinning with satisfaction, she hopped off of Salt and pulled him up next to her. Childlike, her mind was racing with possibilities for this impromptu little tea party. "You suck it now, Salt," she said, sitting primly on her knees. He looked at her uncertainly, then grinned and shrugged. She'd known that Salt would always be game for a mind-fuck, and she also knew that her newfound perversions held him under their spell. So under Katharine's direction, the first man's mouth was removed for Salt's, which tentatively circled Michel's head before finding a rhythm and taking it deeper. She splayed out on the grass and began to masturbate, watching in fascination as Salt crouched at Michel's feet and sucked, as the two other men hotly veered towards an orgasm behind them. Michel held his eyes open now, and they flashed occasionally, as if they were poorly wired to his fury. It was as if he wanted to curse her but couldn't find the force. The sight of her so beautiful and masturbating in the grass, the feel of a wet mouth tonguing him towards orgasm – he was hypnotized and simply could not budge.

A woman with curly, blonde hair and enormous, pale breasts flopped down next to Katharine and playfully kissed her on the cheek. "You're hot!" she giggled. "So come with me. My girlfriend and I want to lick your pussy." Katharine giggled right back and scampered after the woman, bored with the boys now. Just across the lawn they came upon a group of women, all licking in an uninterrupted chain. The large-breasted woman pulled her down to the ground and her waiting friend, who could have been her twin, and they licked Katharine together for a while, each one up its own labia, tongues meeting to flitter together over her clitoris. Eventually Katharine's mouth sought its own new taste, and she slowly crawled along the ground, the women licking behind her, until she found a cunt to sample and they were all joined into the unbroken chain.

Eventually there were men at the edges of the circle, and she held the large-breasted woman tight in her arms, kissing her passionately as a man they couldn't see alternated strokes between the paired eyes of their pussies. Then the woman had disappeared somewhere, and Katharine found herself with another man, who was gentle and licked her pussy as she sucked his cock. At some point she ran across Salt again, still bounding from one pleasure to the next, and she asked if he'd seen Michel. "I think he fled," Salt said wryly. "Although I will not allow my tongue to take the blame for that. The thought! No, it was Selena who finally did him in, I believe. She got her legs around him and started talking filthy, and I got the impression he just sort of short circuited. Sorry about that."

"It's for the best," Katharine said with a grin. Salt skipped off, and she nodded to another man in the shadows, who promptly stepped forward. "So what's your name?" she asked, dropping to her knees. She could not suck enough cock. She sucked and she fucked past all limits of human endurance, and then sometime near dawn, she drifted off in a heap of discarded bodies and slept.

The sun was beginning to rise when she stirred. She felt eyes on her and opened hers to discover a woman whom she had not seen at the orgy looking down upon her. The woman wore a red dress and a floppy red hat. She was curvy and beautiful and was extending her hand. "Maybe we should go someplace a little cozier to talk," she said, and before Katharine could get her bearings, she found herself in the backseat of a comfortable sedan. "Home," Anita said to the driver, and almost immediately Katharine fell asleep on the woman's soft shoulder.

CHAPTER TEN

Katharine awoke in a large, soft bed in one of the most luxuriously feminine rooms she had ever set eyes upon. Everywhere there was ornate Louis Quatorze furniture – chairs, cupboards, and tables covered with exquisitely crafted mementos. Light filtered through the sheer white curtains that fell over two windows across the room. Katherine rose, naked, and walked over to them.

She was on the second floor of an enormous chateau, she discovered, and vaguely recalled seeing signs for Poissy, a town just outside of Paris, early that morning as she had dozed on Anita's shoulder. There was a vast lawn with a long drive that disappeared over a rise. Cypresses lined the drive, and beyond them was a thick forest.

"How did you sleep?" asked a voice behind her. She turned, and framed in the bathroom doorway was a breathtaking feminine form. Yes, she had seen the photos, but even those photos couldn't compare. Anita's skin was naturally brown, her breasts were full and firm, her hips were out of the Renaissance, her black hair waved down over her shoulders, and she had an absolutely bewitching lipsticked smile. "I thought you'd never wake up. Just *look* at you. Taking your clothes off this morning I couldn't believe my eyes, but *now?* You are a vision."

Katharine stammered, and for the first time in what seemed like forever, she felt herself blush. Finally she giggled in embarrassment and said: "I had no idea orgies were so exhausting."

"They *are*, aren't they," Anita laughed. "So come back to bed, darling. Juliette is bringing us up some breakfast." Katharine hesitated for a moment, still overcome by the woman's beauty – by *Anita*, for whom she had been searching day and night, and to whom – now that she had found her – there seemed to be absolutely nothing to say. But Anita was daintily sliding beneath a sheet, so Katharine followed her into bed. The woman promptly scooted over and put a friendly arm around Katharine's shoulder. As she did, her eyes didn't leave Katharine's pert breasts, and she reverently reached out to place her hand over one for a light caress. Then this Juliette – beautiful too, although skinnier and with her blonde hair cut in a short bob – was bringing in a tray heaped with croissants. She was dressed in a maid's black outfit with an unusually short skirt, and she set down the tray on a table at Anita's side of the bed. "Will that be all, Anita?"

"I'm tempted to say no, Juliette," Anita said, "but yes, I think that will be all for now." So Juliette glided out of the room, and Anita leaned over to pour coffee and milk into cups from silver pitchers. She passed a cup to Katharine, and they drank in comfortable silence. Anita delicately ripped croissants into bites for them to eat, and soon Katharine felt completely restored, as well as the luckiest girl in the world.

"I've been wanting to meet you," Anita said after a while. "Reports of your beauty have not been exaggerated, to say the least."

"I've been wanting to meet you, too," Katharine sighed, forcing herself to look up into the depthless black pools of the woman's eyes.

"Did you amuse yourself last night? John Salt wasn't too much of a beast, was he?"

"It was wonderful. Filthy, but wonderful. I needed that more than you can imagine. And Salt? No, he was wonderful, too. I guess you could say that I've come around to his charms."

"He's persuasive that way, isn't he?"

"You know there are so many things I've been wanting to ask you," Katharine interrupted. "About Nicolas, whom you saw at Harriet's gallery that night, and the book, and all these things that have been happening, and…well….”

“They don’t seem to matter so much anymore now that we’re here together in bed, do they?”

“No,” Katharine said with a laugh, nodding to herself. “They don’t.”

“Come here. Come into my arms, beautiful.” Hearing this, finally hearing this, Katharine flung herself into Anita’s embrace like a little girl, and shyly, gloriously, they kissed. They kissed for what seemed like hours, and to Katharine it just felt so *romantic*. She was enthralled by the woman’s lips, and by her body too, which she caressed when the sheet slipped from it. Her breasts, her belly, her hips – Katharine could not touch the woman enough. Anita returned the caresses ardently, kissing Katharine’s nipples, eventually moving down to gently lick at her pussy. Katharine felt as if she was still dreaming, and she stretched her arms over her head to luxuriate in the feeling of Anita’s body moving over hers.

How many days passed in that room? Or was it just hours? They flirted with the edge between reality and dreams until they slipped over and dozed for a bit. When Katharine opened her eyes, she saw that Anita had risen to step over to a makeup table with a mirror that reflected her shining face back to Katharine, who watched longingly as the woman opened a drawer and drew out what looked like two penises.

Anita looked reverently at the object and turned to show it to Katharine, who saw now that the two cocks were connected at their bases and jutted out eight or nine inches in either direction from a thick rubber bulge. The fleshy pink color of the thing was perfect, and no detail had been ignored. There was that hard vein tracing the base of each cock, and the thinner blued veins snaking over their lengths.

"It's incredible," Katharine whispered as Anita handed it to her to feel.

"I'll show you how it works," Anita said, easing down onto the bed next to Katharine. "Hand it to me." She took it and lay back on the bed, splaying her thighs so that the pink line of her pussy was fully exposed through her tangle of dark hair. "Like this," she murmured, holding the instrument with two hands, one of the arrowed rubber heads hovering just above her labia. Spiraling the head down towards her opening, she gently circled those lips aside, exposing the wet surfaces inside. Katharine watched in a sort of rapture as the tip of the penis entered and went deeper, angled down and then back up into the warm embrace of Anita's cunt. Soon the first cock had been inserted all the way up to the knob that separated it from the second. Anita's sex had swallowed it whole, and her lips were puckered kiss-like around the object.

"Now," Anita sighed, breathless with passion. "This middle part here is flexible, so you can bend it in any direction. See? I can lie with it in my cunt and the other prick sticking straight up. I can even masturbate like a man." She chuckled at this and began to stroke the second, now "erect" cock that protruded from her. It was so realistic that it seemed to have become a living part of her, a perfect cock that lacked only balls. Anita snarled manfully, like a cowboy or a gangster, and stroked her new appendage as if this was an old habit of hers. But the easy amusement soon drifted from her face, and with wide eyes and a slack mouth, she stroked.

"Fantastic, isn't it?" she said after a while. "You can even walk around the room with it." With this she rocked up off the bed and paraded around the bedroom with her new fantastic member jutting out from her cunt, holding it proudly in one hand as if she were the world's biggest stud. It was the most incongruously beautiful sight Katharine had ever seen - Anita's perfect body be-cocked.

"It's fun to strut," Anita said, flopping down onto the bed again, "but of course that's hardly the point. Come over here and sit on me. Let me show you." Katharine hopped up on her knees and let herself be drawn into Anita's inviting arms. Straddling her, Katharine presented her bare pussy to the jutting rubber penis. As she squatted, her labia parted greedily, and the rubber dong squished up into her. She felt it bore its way into her center, and she shuddered. Then she slowly extended her legs until the women lay thigh to thigh, belly to belly, breast to breast.

"Now move," the dark beauty commanded. "Fuck me. You have a cock now too, so show me how you use it." Smiling shyly, Katharine obeyed. The technique took a moment to master. At first she was afraid that if she rose up off of Anita, then the rubber would slip out of her, but it was wide and well-suctioned inside, and Anita knew just how to thrust gently forward herself, preventing either one of their pussies from pulling back further than halfway down their respective shafts. Occasionally when they were simultaneously over-come with need, their cunts would meet at the center and their labia would wetly smooch.

"Now roll over onto your side." Katharine did as she was told. She would have walked on fire for Anita, she would have driven off cliffs. As she turned, she again feared that the dildo would spurt out of her, but Anita rolled expertly onto her side at the same moment, maintaining their parallel connec-tion. "See?" Anita said. "Two horny lovers like us? You just don't disconnect. We can even dance and stay like one. Let me show you." With this she rolled on top of Katharine, put her arms around her and lunged back until they were both standing. And then they tangoed, cheek to cheek, breast to breast, Katharine's long, trained legs scissoring across the room, accompanying Anita's legs, which were just as long and just as agile. Katharine cried out in delight. "This day! Wonderful Anita! Thank you. It really is fabulous to dance with you like this."

When they came to the mirror over the makeup table, Anita stopped their dancing and turned away from Katharine so that they could both look into the mirror. *Like Siamese twins,* Katharine thought to herself, *joined at the hip.* She marveled again at the Hollywood beauty of Anita, and then she found that she was marveling at herself. She was beautiful too, terribly beautiful – those lips, those breasts. What a woman that was in the mirror! What confidence she now had, but then confidence wasn't the word. Confidence was a way of forcing yourself upon the world, but now Katharine *was* the world. *Siamese twins.*

Still cocked together, Anita guided them back to the bed, where they hugged again and fell together to the soft mattress. Completely uninhibited now, her eyes shining reverently, as if taking a holy sacrament, Katharine clasped Anita's body tightly. Gently she sought the beauty's yielding lips and kissed them with an open-mouthed passion that was indistinguishable from love.

"Darling," she murmured, a word that had never before escaped her lips. "Darling Anita." In her extensive bedroom wisdom, Anita knew what was happening, and she returned the love, softly at first, then fiercely, breaking off kisses only to let Katharine cry out another loving term of affection. Their fucking had fully begun.

Their bodies wriggled against each other, Katharine on top, and then somehow, with magical erotic ease, Anita on top, fucking away, bringing Katharine steadily towards the climax that Anita knew would also be her own. Anita now lifted her torso by straightening her arms – like a man supports himself – drawing their bodies apart so that they could fuck each other deeper, pulling apart out to the edges of their rubber joint, then plunging back again so that their cunts squished together. From moments of ferocity they moved into lazier stretches, slowly grinding against one another and kissing. Then their hands would become more urgent again, their kisses almost angry, and then they both felt it coming upon them.

Katharine had never known a climax like this, and she ached for its bliss to last forever. Arching up into the woman who bestrode her, she clasped at her curves, hugging her so tightly that she felt as if all of her would flow, body and soul, deep into Anita. She took and she gave, crying tears of joy, murmuring bliss. Anita smiled down at her like a loving conqueror. Yes, Katharine was made for men, but now and for the rest of her life, she would also look for love in the eyes of women. Anita knew this, because she had once been Katharine, and she had discovered this love for herself.

"God you're magnificent!" Anita gloated down on her. And then it was over. Utterly exhausted the two women slid apart to lie on their sides, still linked by the dildo. In the angled afternoon light filtering through the sheer curtains, they both fell asleep.

Was it another hour later that Katharine awoke? She sat up in bed as if she had been startled, a single word on her lips: *Love*. Anita was sitting on a chair across the room and pulling on pants. She watched amusedly as Katharine struggled to form a sentence: "Harriet said I had to get out of the book, and I think this is what she meant."

"Yes," Anita chuckled.

"The book was the homework," Katharine continued, gathering steam. "But I've learned my lesson and am not going to take refuge in homework anymore. I even *recognized* something in you that I've never seen in anyone, and I think you recognized it in me too. *Recognitions*. That's crazy Switch talking. What about Nicolas? Oh please tell me more about all of these people, Anita."

"Let's not worry about them now, beautiful. There will be time. Now let's take a walk while we still have the sun." So

Katharine dressed too, in a pair of jeans and a casual button-down shirt that Anita had lain out for her and which fit perfectly. They went downstairs and out onto the front lawn, then made for the trees, where a path appeared that took them down to a stream. Sunlight blinked through the trees as they strolled along the gurgling water, occasionally holding hands. Anita pointed out the different varieties of vegetation, pausing occasionally to pick a blackberry to pop into Katharine's mouth, then chase it with a kiss. The fresh air rejuvenated Katharine after the day's lazy fucking, and when they arrived back at the chateau their bath had already been poured.

In the bathroom Anita undressed her and guided her down into the suds before undressing herself. "Now we need to get you ready," she purred, squeezing into the tub behind Katharine, straddling her with her legs to soap her shoulders, neck and breasts. Katharine sighed as Anita soaped all over, paying particularly gentle attention to her submerged pussy, which was slightly sore but immensely satisfied. After the bath Anita dried her off with great attentiveness, pressing the thick towel to every inch of her body. She sat her down on a stool and patiently brushed her hair. She perfumed her neck and led her back out into the bedroom, where two dresses had been lain out.

"Your choice," Anita said, and Katharine chose a red one not unlike the dress that Anita had worn the night before. It fit perfectly, Katharine was again astonished to discover.

As Anita pulled the other dress down over her shoulders, Katharine looked at herself in the mirror and marveled again. Yes, she really was that curvy. She really was that sexy, little Katharine Bright.

Anita appeared in the mirror beside her, another wonder. "Ooh, sexy," she purred approvingly. "So I think we're just about ready."

CHAPTER ELEVEN

Juliette had changed into a black suit with a snappy driver's cap and stopped the car in front of Cleopatra's Dream before hopping out to open the back door for Anita and Katharine.

"What are we doing *here?*" Katharine couldn't help but ask, but Anita just looped an arm around hers and led her into the theater. Beyond the metal door the heavy curtains had been pulled aside, revealing a lobby that Katharine had not noticed on her first visit. The lobby was crowded with people in formal dress. They parted like a sea when Anita and Katharine appeared, and as the women walked towards the center of the room, men and women of astonishing elegance – sharp tuxedos and glittering dresses – stepped forward to greet them. "You're like a queen," Katharine nervously whispered in Anita's ear, still completely clueless as to what they were doing at the mysterious strip club, but Anita just laughed. "Darling, *you're* the queen," she said. "These people are all here for *you.*"

And it was true. They all seemed to know her. "Welcome, Katharine," said one after another, each more interesting looking than the last. As she shook hands and smiled, utterly bewildered, she spotted Harriet talking in a group across the lobby and nodded. Harriet winked, and Katharine felt her heart flutter. It wasn't until she saw Switch Reno, flanked by Toto and a stunning woman almost a head taller than them both, that she began to suspect the purpose of their gathering. These were The Known.

Anita had drifted off to tantalize some admirers when Katharine felt a kiss at her ear. A hand reached around her to offer a full glass of champagne, and she turned to find Salt's beaming face just a few inches from her own. "I figured you could use a drink," he drawled. "Are you ready for this?"

"Ready for *what*, Salt?" she whispered, downing half the glass. "Is this some meeting of *The Known*."

"God I hate that name," he sighed. "And you know that old line: I wouldn't want to be a part of any club that would have me as its member. But here I am. When sex is involved I'm willing to make *all* exceptions. Speaking of which, how's Michel?"

"I have no idea. I haven't seen him and doubt I ever will again."

"You're welcome," he said, and as nervous as she was, she couldn't help but laugh. He took her hand, and they looked around the room together. *So this is the secret orgy club,* she thought. Salt's hand in hers was surprisingly calming, and she let herself really examine the faces in the room. As she did, she began to notice that something *was* unusual about them. Eyes were lit up by conversations, bodies moved with confident ease, hands lingered on arms. Maybe it was just the effect of her day with Anita, but it struck her that everybody seemed to be in love with everybody else.

Then the lights in the lobby began to blink. "Ooh goody," Salt said. "The show's about to start. I've got to find Selena, but I'll see you in there." Which left Katharine standing alone again, made more nervous than ever by all the people who seemed to know her and want to kiss her cheek or shake her hand. Finally she was rescued by Anita, who took her arm again to lead her into the theater. Anita's extreme silence was unnerving now, and Katharine begged: "Anita, please tell me what's going on? Why is everyone looking at me?"

Anita paused and turned to kiss her deeply on the mouth. After a long moment she pulled her radiant face away and said: "Darling, this is your initiation. It's normal to be nervous, but please trust me. Do not fight against the moment, and let yourself be led." Then she squeezed her arm and cried: "I'm so excited!"

They walked down the aisle to the front row with every eye upon them and sat in two empty seats. After a moment the overhead lights dimmed and spotlights illuminated the stage, where the only decoration was a single large bed.

Once the crowd had silenced themselves, a man appeared from one of the wings and stepped up to the edge of the stage. Katharine's heart skipped a beat. The man was Nessim, beautiful Nessim, and he was staring straight at her. Not a sound could be heard as he tore his eyes from hers to glance out over the crowd and say: "Ladies and gentlemen, we are gathered here tonight to celebrate Katharine Bright."

At this Katharine put a hand to her mouth and hissed in Anita's ear: *"I'm not ready for this, Anita!"*

"Darling," Anita purred reassuringly, "if anyone has ever been ready for this, it's you. Just relax and enjoy it." Nessim was staring down at her again with those endless olive eyes, and she understood that she was meant to go up to the stage and join him. Tentatively she rose and slowly made her way up the steps. As she approached, Nessim reached out and embraced her. Her legs almost gave way as he planted a wet, lingering kiss on her lips. After a long moment he pulled away, leaving her lips hungering after his.

Turning to the crowd again, he said: "This is Katharine Bright, and she is known to us." Wild applause. Katharine had never felt so glorified in all of her life. She looked out

across the faces in that room where she had once been overwhelmed by the dancing Brigitte, and she saw all the faces
that had accompanied her along her journey, beaming back
in admiration: Harriet, Toto, Switch, Salt, Selena, Anita, and
even Neema, Nessim's stunning secretary, who now rose
from her chair and proceeded up to the stage. She took her
place beside Katharine and whispered in her ear: "Are you
ready?" Katharine nodded, and Neema motioned for her to
follow over to the bed. The crowd had fallen silent again and
watched the scene with rapt attention.

"Do you want the blindfold or not," Neema asked once they
had reached the edge of the bed. Katharine looked out across
the darkened sea of faces and said: "I'd better take it."

"I did too," Neema said with a smile, and she took a strip of
black silk from the bed to tie around Katharine's head. When
Katharine's eyes were banded, Neema whispered again: "Let
us see you now, my lovely. I'll help you with your zipper."
Katharine nodded as she felt the zipper come down at the
side of her dress, and then it was being helped over her head.
More wild applause.

"Oh darling," Neema said. "They adore you. *I* adore you.
Now let's let them see those legendary breasts." With this she
whipped Katharine's bra from her so abruptly that her tits
bounced, and then she leaned and slipped off her underwear

for good measure. Katharine was now entirely naked, and the applause was delirious. "Turn," Neema whispered, so close that Katharine was made dizzy by the woman's seductive scent, and so she turned, displaying her ass to The Known, who appreciated it as much as they had the rest of her.

"Now lie down," Neema said, and again Katharine obeyed, blindly, letting herself be eased back onto the soft sweep of the mattress. Neema left her with a quick kiss that Katharine, despite her nervousness and disorientation, wished she could have prolonged, and then music began to play – opera serenading Katharine's perfect naked form. She had no idea what might happen next, but she had already resolved to take Anita's advice and live in the moment, letting herself be carried along by circumstances, which were admittedly unbearably exciting.

The crowd began to murmur. She lay there for what seemed like hours. Then she felt someone kiss her foot. The crowd fell silent as foot became calf, became knee, became thigh. The kisses on her thigh soon moved up to her pussy, where the kisses lingered until she was squirming. Strangely enough, the thought of being watched beyond the blindfold only excited her more. Her pleasure was the star of this show, and she wanted to feel it completely. Whose tongue was at her ever-blossoming bud? Neema's, Nessim's, Anita's, Salt's? Her conclusion? It didn't matter in the slightest because she was in love with them all.

The kisses moved to her hips, her belly, her breasts, and only then did she feel that it was a naked man against her, with long, lithe muscles and a firm cock pressed against her thigh. Well that would do just fine, she thought, as the man kissed her nipples and made her sigh. Then her collar bone, attentively, her neck, *oh*, her cheek. The man smelled wonderfully, and she fixed her hands to his hard, churning ass to pull him into her as he kissed: her jaw, her ear, her lips, lips, lips, lips. "I want to *see* you," she cried out. "This is my dream, and whoever you are, I want to *see* you, and I want them to see us, too."

Gently then, she felt the man's hands at the back of her head, undoing the blindfold. Slowly, he slid it out from under her hair.

And then her eyes opened, and the only thing that surprised her was how little surprised she was. She had been dreaming about this for months, after all, and there with his incomparable body pressed to hers, was Nicolas Lenoir.

"I'm sorry," he said with that infectious grin, his face just inches from hers. Was the crowd applauding again? She had no idea. There was only the two of them in the world.

"Well that was quite a seduction, Mister Lenoir," she murmured, grinning right back, eyes shining. "Couldn't you have just asked me back to your place for a nightcap and put on some sexy music?"

"Why do I have the feeling that wouldn't have worked?"

"Well…. Maybe it wouldn't have. In any case, I forgive you." He hovered over her as if uncertain of what to do next. "Oh lover," she said. "I'm thoroughly seduced and everybody's waiting, so just put your arms around me and fuck me quick."

Which is exactly what he did.

Available in Winter 2011

The Sex Experiment 2011

All of the best experiments of 2011 elegantly presented in a special collector's yearbook.

Each experiment is accompanied by a beautiful black & white photograph of the elusive mrs. x.

www.experimentalbooks.com

www.ingramcontent.com/pod-product-compliance
Lightning Source LLC
Chambersburg PA
CBHW070814120626
46556CB00002B/500